Hope you enjoy!

THE UNEXPECTED OCCURRENCE
OF THADDEUS HOBBLE

Gareth Wiley

—X—

BY THE SAME AUTHOR

I Am Dead

Icon's Request

A Matter of Dark

Where the Birds Hide at Night

So far…

THE UNEXPECTED OCCURRENCE OF THADDEUS HOBBLE

A BRIEF HISTORY OF THE GREAT COLLECTIVE

GARETH WILES

Matador
9 Priory Business Park,
Wistow Road, Kibworth Beauchamp,
Leicestershire. LE8 0RX
Tel: (+44) 116 279 2299
Fax: (+44) 116 279 2277
Email: books@troubador.co.uk
Web: www.troubador.co.uk/matador

ISBN 978 1784622 343

British Library Cataloguing in Publication Data.
A catalogue record for this book is available from the British Library.

Printed and bound in the UK by TJ International, Padstow, Cornwall
Typeset in 11pt Book Antiqua by Troubador Publishing Ltd, Leicester, UK

Matador is an imprint of Troubador Publishing Ltd

MIX
Paper from
responsible sources
FSC   FSC® C013056
www.fsc.org

For my father, 'Gwynny'

I would also like to pay special thanks to Mark 'Geeks' Longman and Phil Reading, who have both shown tireless dedication to and appreciation of me and my work. Their devotion shows no signs of ceasing…

PART ONE

THE GREAT COLLECTIVE

1580

At the end of the chalky stone lane, and beyond the dew-drizzled blossoming oak trees, lay a water well. It was here, deep in Myrtle Forest, that puzzlement was the order of the day – for, this water well was in the queerest of locations. Secreted beyond a sensible distance from the village, and disguised in dense lichen, its water served no being. Who had built it, and why, would remain an unknown. Happen that a young lad presently ran up to it; not for water, but to toss a monetary gift down it and make a wish. The mousy young thing was but five years of age, and straying far from where he belonged. It was no matter, because no danger would ever occur to him out here. The well was known only to him, and would grant wishes only to him. He wished to live eternally. He wished to know all there was to know.

'Peter,' called his mother in a shrill wail, emerging in her drab grey gown from some dense fern foliage in the distance. The boy sought to hide his well, knowing it would no longer grant his wishes if the old girl was to discover its existence. A dash in the opposite direction set the spring growth swinging about him, calling Mother's attention away from his secret. It was damp underfoot, but not slippery, and the elder's longer legs soon caught up with the little boy. She hoisted him into the air and howled with victory: 'You are the devil himself, child! But, you cannot outwit your own mother. I always find you.' Her hair was grey, though she was not old, and her face creased in all manner of directions as she grinned. Peter's long brown hair lay greasily still like a wig as the rest of his head thrashed violently about in the struggle. It was no good, she was too strong for him. Though some part of him yearned for freedom in its purest form, he adored this about her – she was completely dominant over him, completely in charge. The little boy could rest easy in her bosom, fully protected by her unrivalled strength from any horrors that the outside world threw up. Nature was freedom, humanity was imprisonment.

* * *

Mother tossed a smelly dark lump of scrag end into the skillet above the fireplace, shielding her face as the hot brown water splashed up. There came a knock at the door and it presently opened. In hobbled Beckett the doctor, his bent cane supporting his vast swollen frame. His plethora of chins wobbled as he swished his black coat at Peter, who dodged out of the way and went to hide in the corner of the sparse room. He didn't like Beckett the doctor – he was a difficulty in the little boy's eyes. Nevertheless Mother was here, and Mother would protect him.

'Good day to you, Mrs Smith. I bring news of your extinguished husband's debts,' the obesity gobbled delightfully, his pinprick eyes moistening as Mother fumbled about in her pockets.

'I had some coins to pay you, good Doctor, I did,' she wailed, the sweat pouring from her brow. Peter looked sheepish, knowing full well that he'd taken his mother's coins and thrown them down the well.

'You appear to be struggling to locate the payment I am owed, Mrs Smith,' Beckett purred, licking his lips as he stepped closer and took hold of her arm with his stubby red fingers. 'I am sure we can think up some way of paying your late husband's debts.' He stroked the erect hair on her arm. Suddenly she dropped to her knees and then flat on her face as Beckett stepped back. 'Oh dear, she is taken down with illness,' he mumbled vaguely.

Peter ran to his mother and tried frantically to waken her, but she would not move. Reluctantly, Beckett struggled down and lifted her arm.

'Mother!' Peter cried.

'Your mother is dead, child,' he sighed.

The little boy shot out of there and dashed away from the ramshackle house as quickly as his tiny legs would allow.

* * *

Peter reached the well and, clasping its stone rim, pulled himself up to peer down inside.

'Bring her back,' he demanded, 'bring back Mother.'

He dropped again to the ground and ran from the well, back home.

* * *

A number of folks from the village had gathered around the house by the time Peter got back. Two men were carrying the body out of the door as he stepped forward and made a grab for its limp hand. All at once it firmed up and clasped him back. Her eyes opened and she gave out a deep breath. The two horrified men dropped her and recoiled as loud whispers quickly spread amongst the onlookers.

'The dead rises,' Beckett gasped. 'This can mean only one thing...'

'Witch!' one of the neighbours yelled in fear.

'She hath the devil within her,' Beckett screeched. 'We must purge her of this wickedness.'

* * *

Mother sobbed and tugged at the tight rope bonds keeping her fixed to the pole as they tore into her flesh. A toothy old woman held a screaming little Peter back as a villager set some sticks beneath Mother alight. The fire spread quickly, melting the woman's hair and skin off. Eventually her deafening cries for mercy ceased, and her engulfed body went limp. Mania swept through the crowd of onlookers as they roared with burning happiness. The fire went on as Peter managed to pull away and run from this awful place.

* * *

He came back to the well and, in a total fit of despair, threw himself down it. His little body plopped into the water below and he took in a huge mouthful of it. Suddenly, however, a small wooden door in the wall of the well swung open and a pair of hands reached out to Peter and pulled him up. Once lifted through the door, he was dropped and left as the person scurried away. The boy stayed on his knees in the darkness, his wet hands sticking to the soil floor, as a group of hooded figures appeared before him in this dingy recess. They huddled together in the darkness and mumbled to one another. After a moment or two, they dispersed and one approached him.

'We are The Great Collective – we are a gathering of higher minds. We know who you are, Master Smith, and what you are capable of. You brought your own mother back from the dead. You, small child, are of a higher level like us. You will join us.'

1596

Peter was twenty-one when the large upright box first appeared in The Great Collective's secret meeting hall. It must have come there by itself, for it was too big to have been brought through the small inconspicuous entrance. It was black – a glossy black – and did nothing but stand there. The skinny young man squinted and arched his tall frame forward, his short-sighted eyes not quite sure of the box's presence. Circling it, he hesitatingly brushed his floppy mousy hair aside and moved closer. He wanted to touch it, but couldn't. It was the only thing he didn't feel superior to. The Great Collective had certainly filled him with a sense of self-assurance. The life they'd provided for him, the only life he had ever known, was one of constant deviousness and doubt. They lived separately from the rest of the villagers, putting doubt in his mind about everything the outside world stood for – family, religion... humans as the pinnacle of creation. He believed as they believed, that humanity was an insignificant part of a much vaster universe of beings. Earth had been left in the corner, forgotten. Now that this box was here, Peter felt more than ever that the teachings he had received were correct.

Peter could see the beginning and the end – at the start there was absolutely nothing save for a phantasmal gouging of emptiness, but then all at once a tremendous explosion so vast as to be incomprehensible set forth a scattering of dust holding the very materials for the birth of life until that same dust, moving and moving further apart on its journey, got too distant and too apart that it ceased to be and became nothing once more.

'What are you, where are you from?' he asked it.

Another of the collective entered – an older man with an auburn parting and tight skin. 'What is that?' he called out, wide nostrils dilating at the foot of his long nose. Peter could not take his eyes from the box. Literally, he could not move. It would not allow him.

'Darren,' Peter addressed his fellow, 'I am overcome by It.'

'It,' Darren mumbled, he too now drawn by the power of the box.

'I can feel It within me, I can hear It,' Peter gasped, the culmination of the entirety of universal existence washing through his mind like a vast ungraspable behemoth. Instantly he knew all there was to know, and could see all there was to see. It was The Space, and It had delivered Itself here – open and unending for Peter and the others to peer inside. The box was both there and not there at the same time, willing to be seen by those who wanted to see. That The Space appeared to have a physical presence was but a human impression, the only way It could be understood and reasoned by these ape-variants.

* * *

The Great Collective – forever pompous, eternally seeing what they believed others could not see – had struck it lucky. That The Space had appeared only to them was accepted as divination, and with all the trappings that brought was treated with more right than privilege. They gathered around their meeting place now, Peter and Darren as their new leading forces, to try to comprehend what had occurred. The room was in complete silence, yet it drowned in a hellish din. This came not from vocals of the mouth, but thoughts in their minds. Every thought that crossed those minds could be heard by the others, and each one could hear the minds of every other living being elsewhere. It was a cacophony of madness, stopped only by a recoiling from The Space. But, the lure was too great – to grab hold of infinity was the reward for embracing It.

'I can hear The Space,' Peter addressed the gathering around him.

'We can *all* hear The Space,' Darren called over him. 'It allows us all a portal into whatever we so wish.'

'It is so clear and yet so vague,' Peter sighed, unable to fully comprehend the situation. He had a portal into endlessness, yet felt he was hitting a wall. At once he stiffened up, his eyes glazing over as his body shook. 'The Space is beckoning me to deliver Its gift onto us all,' he uttered. 'Immortality. We all shall never cease to be.'

'Eternal existence?' Darren mused rather stoically. 'Quite a useful occurrence.'

1600

The rich man was down on his knees, his lace gown splattered and sodden with mud as Darren danced before him. The jolly man, his floppy auburn hair flapping about as his feet swiftly slipped and sloshed in the mud, roared with laughter. He held no weapon, and no other person was present to restrain the rich man. He was utterly fixed there by forces unseen, terror writ large on his increasingly greying face. Darren presently kicked a heel of mud into that face, and the man was unable to move his hands to wipe it away. He bent down and took a coin purse from the rich victim's pocket, jingling it about as his happiness increased. 'You dunce, you dolt!' Darren cackled. Suddenly he stopped and looked ahead into the distance. Peter was marching towards him, thunder torn across his face.

'No!' Peter yelled, 'this cannot take place. Not now, not ever!'

'Why not, you fool?' Darren called back. 'We have the power to control whomever we so wish. The merest thought of keeping this buffoon fixed to the ground and it occurs!'

'We cannot abuse The Space.'

Darren thought otherwise, pocketing the coin purse and dashing away. This released the sitting duck from the terrible grip and he further collapsed in a heap of shock.

1611

'Tis a job well done, Bill,' Peter praised the man beside him as they walked out of The Globe. He smiled back. 'Thank you for helping me write it. It is as though you can pluck entire tomes of brilliance from nowhere and deliver them straight to me.'

Suddenly a group of witch hunters appeared, grabbing Peter. 'Good day, Mr Shakespeare,' they said to the older gentleman, doffing their hats. They dragged Peter away.

* * *

'All these men are guilty of terrible evils against our pure and honest existence,' the head of the witch hunt called out. 'I personally oversaw their capture from across the country to bring them back to Myrtleville to be punished for their sins.' He looked across at the long line of men standing with rope around their necks and their hands bound behind their backs. Peter, amongst them, sported a big grin on his face. 'You call yourselves The Great Collective, you profess to possess immortality.'

'The Space has granted us thus,' Peter yelled back confidently.

'Then let us all bear witness today to the miracle of endless life!'

'We allow our ends to occur to prove to you our return,' Darren called out.

The villagers roared with laughter as a lever was pulled and the floor beneath each of the men disappeared. They dropped, suspended only by the rope around their broken necks. They dangled there silently like runner beans waiting to be picked.

1630

To all intents and purposes, The Great Collective ended that day in 1611. There was no miracle of dead bodies rising from their graves, nor was there any other sign of the immortality those men had so sworn by. Minutes passed, hours passed – days, months and then years. Many years. They were quickly forgotten, as such people are, and Myrtleville carried on as before. It was in 1630 when a young mother, never having known of the past hangings, gave birth to Peter Smith. This wasn't just another Peter Smith, but the *same* Peter Smith. He had been reborn.

1651

'Why are you so terribly shy with girls, Peter?'

'I am not shy with you, Mother,' the young man replied.

'That is because I am not a girl – I am a woman, and *your* mother.'

'I am close to you, for I have never really had a mother before,' was his response. He then thought about what he'd said, and wished he hadn't.

'What a peculiar thing to say, Peter.' The woman looked back at her son and for a brief moment wondered who he was – not that she had gone senile, but that she could not see her son sitting before her. She'd certainly given birth to the baby that had grown into the man that was in her company presently, but he seemed to her something else than that; not necessarily something more, just something else. 'You have always had a mother – me.'

'In this life, yes; but not before.' The young man knew all about what his prior self had lived through, what his mother and he had suffered. Death would have relinquished the mulling over of such awful things. Peter Smith was not dead, however – The Space had seen to that.

'Peter, really, you *must* stop this nonsense about a prior life,' Mother snapped angrily. 'There is only one life for each of us, and it is here and now. It is holding you back, you are not making the most of your time with all this contemplation. You must get yourself into the world and make a life with a woman, and achieve.'

'Achieve what?'

Mother could not answer, for she knew not what. It was for Peter himself to decide what he wanted to achieve in life. Still, simply surviving could be deemed an achievement all of its own in these times. He somehow felt, having already lived before, that he could relax this time around and muse over what he wanted to accomplish in future lives. He had plenty of time – endless time – to do as he wished. He did not need to be forthcoming with the opposite sex. Things would sort themselves out.

1666

'You are not the first Peter Smith to live in Myrtleville.'

'A common name.'

'You share his name and his personality, and yet...' but the old woman petered off.

'And yet *what*, hag? Speak up, move your rotten old tongue.'

'And yet I saw Peter Smith hanged here in the year 1611. I was a young girl, but I remember it clearly. You were so confident you would return to life.'

'And I did. I was born again – I have lived my entire life again.' He looked rather glum as he turned from the old woman. 'The same people who murdered me stood by and watched as my mother burned alive when I was but a boy,' he grumbled.

'That was the way of things back then, we are trying to change for the better,' she replied gingerly.

'I have witnessed just as much evil in this life as I did in my original life. Humanity will never change.'

'It will, my boy, it will!' she replied with such conviction. Peter turned to face her again, wanting desperately to believe her. She smiled warmly.

'I wished for eternal life, I wanted to know all there was to know – I was granted both. The Space has shown me all that ever was, is or will be and it fills me with dread. Tell me, old one, how can I use my position to do good in the world?'

'You must seek out the good in others and emulate it,' were her simple words.

'And if I can find no good?'

'Then you are correct, and humanity's course is predestined to disaster.' With this, she shuffled away and Peter would never see her again. He was getting used to never seeing people again. Some, of course, he saw too much of.

He thought back to his original life, and he remembered it well. His mother had so suffered at the hands of those ordinary villagers and they had all gone unpunished. It was too late to try and seek revenge now – they were all dead, save a minuscule number of the children who were now like the crippled old woman. He had been born again, memory intact, to another mother whose fate had not been so gruesome. He felt guilty that he'd been able to experience a new mother and leave his first life behind. But, it hadn't been left behind – he lived it over and over in his mind. Rebirth felt like a curse. Were he to forget, he could potentially cope with such a burden. Yet, what would be the point if he could not remember from one life to another?

He was now thirty-six, the same age he was when he'd first died. He looked back to 1651, when he was twenty-one, and that reminded him of his first culmination of twenty-one years in 1596. That big upright box had made itself known to The Great Collective, and especially to him, and had opened their minds to some strange entity that seemed to encourage them to name it The Space. It was difficult to decide upon what it actually *was* called, or if indeed it had a name at all. More difficult still was pinpointing what The Space actually was or wanted, but what it provided was certainly what that group of arrogant men had wanted – immortality, complete knowledge. There was too much information to fully appreciate or sort

17

through; it just rushed about in their minds. Still, The Space had certainly come good on its promise of everlasting life as Peter's presence right now proved. There, too, was the potentially devastating tool that allowed control over the mind and body of others. He had witnessed others of the collective deploy it, but he had always sought to shy away from such power. He knew The Space was the culmination of everything that ever was, is or will be, but that in itself felt like a gap – a gap in experience. He wondered what he still had to encounter after two lots of thirty-six years.

Ahead of him stood a very thin, very plain woman. Her long blonde hair lay flat against her head, as did her arms against her body. She was unmoving, unresponsive, as Peter stepped closer. 'Who are you?' he called out to her. 'What do you want?' He called out to The Space for an answer. Silence. It was the first time The Space had declined to give him what he required. He blinked and the woman was gone. Her unremarkable, yet sharply-pointed, face was not in the least bit unpleasant. No, if anything Peter was drawn to it. The anguish of *not* knowing about her after having known all there was to know was what drew him to her. Nonetheless she was no more, and he posited he had imagined her.

'Hath the plague not yet wiped the smirk off thy face?' a voice called out from within the woods behind him. It was the voice of Darren. He stepped out into the open, with three other members of the collective, all dressed in their ritualistic red lace gowns.

'Anthony the silent,' Peter laughed, turning and catching sight of the gathering. 'You were once of the highest order amongst us. Now you cannot utter a single word.'

'His mind is burnt, destroyed by the true intensity of all knowledge,' Darren answered for him. Anthony just stood there, behind Darren as were the other two, with a vacant stare upon his chubby face. He was tall, but bent forward, and he looked like a lost child – ignorant of the future, almost aware of danger.

'And then there is Stephen Noble – Stephen the righteous,' Peter carried on, pointing out the next man behind Darren. He was a dashing young chap with a neatly trimmed beard and looked rather smart in his gown, carrying it better than the others. Without the facial hair he'd have looked almost feminine – his cheeks were smooth and rosy under there – and his brow was soft and rounded. He smiled back at Peter and nodded.

'Ahem,' the third man interjected, clearing his throat and twitching his eye.

'Oh yes, and then Jim… just Jim,' Peter acknowledged the man – who sported a wide open mouth which somewhat appeared to hold up and support a set of drooping eyes – almost as an afterthought. 'What can I do for you all?'

'I shall speak for us, collectively,' Darren started. Peter raised an eyebrow, knowing full well that this person had always been somewhat of a troubling character morally. 'There is concern amongst the collective, and not just us four but others, that you seem to see yourself as our leader.'

'Nonsense,' Peter responded glibly, waving his hand about to illustrate the preposterous nature of Darren's claim. His accusers narrowed their eyes. 'I was, despite perhaps not being the longest serving of the collective, the first to make contact with The Space.'

'Alongside me,' Darren emphasised.

'I did come across the box *first*… not that it matters, of course.'

'We would like to use our skills for gain,' Jim cut in, 'and you would appear not to.'

'Personal gain?' Peter asked. All at once he felt his feet dashing about. He looked down to see that he was dancing like a drunken idiot. 'Stop this,' he bit at them, as Darren and Jim smiled. Stephen looked on contemplatively, whilst Anthony was as blank and as empty as ever.

'Make us stop, why don't you?' Darren goaded. 'Tap into your own power and push us away.'

'Never.'

'Then you will be our puppy,' Jim laughed.

'Pure, perfect Peter the puppy,' Darren cried out in mirth.

Suddenly Peter did stop, and Darren and Jim seemed briefly impressed as they ceased their ribbing. However, the once-dancing one was again drawn to a reappearance of the blonde woman, who was standing behind the four men. Their eyes too became fixed on something behind Peter, and they simultaneously dropped to their knees. He knew the big box was behind him – he could feel Its pulse – but he chose not to turn and face it. The choice of doing anything was quickly removed altogether when he felt a piercing sensation through his chest. It brought him crashing to the ground, dead.

The men were taken somewhat unawares, and Stephen was the first to register unease. 'Stricken down, gone after thirty-six years,' he gulped. 'That was his exact age when last he was taken from this world.'

'What are you saying?' Jim demanded, grabbing hold of Stephen's collars as he instantly felt the weight of the universe struggling to run through his brain.

'You know exactly what I am saying,' Stephen came back at him, pulling away, 'you can see into my mind with The Space's aid.'

'Tis a benefit of fate that all four of us were returned to this world at different times than Peter, and lived various years in our first lives,' Darren mused. 'I came back three years later than he this time, and I was that much older when we first succumbed to the reaping that befell us all in 1611. Does that mean I have a precise set of years left to live this second life?' He looked around at horrified faces. 'Answer me!'

'The Space gifts us all that we wish, up to a point,' Stephen remarked. 'We must try to draw It closer.'

'Tis a horror of horrors!' Jim cried, his face spasming as his twitch intensified. 'I was a youngster then as I am now... will I never see old age?'

Darren's sight fixed on Anthony and it froze there, his brow becoming increasingly less tense. A smirk gradually appeared on his lips. 'There are ways to test our theory, Collective,' he uttered, his eyes still glued on the bulky mute.

'Go on,' Stephen encouraged.

Jim grabbed hold of Darren and shook him in desperation. 'Tell us, tell us!' he shouted. Darren slapped Jim across the face with the back of his hand as he moistened his lips with a hairy tongue.

'If my calculations are correct, then Anthony should outlive all of us. He is the youngest of us now, yet he was even older than I when we hanged,' Darren pointed out.

'So?' Jim replied.

'We should not live to see him die in this life,' Darren responded, bringing out a dagger from inside his coat.

Jim and Stephen stepped back as Darren ran at Anthony and went to thrust the knife into his stomach. But, it would not go all the way. His hand ceased to move, the dagger slipped to the ground and Darren halted right where he was as the unharmed simple man outstretched his hand and took his attacker's to shake it. Darren pulled his hand away, using it instead to smack Anthony across the back of the head. The lad slowly wept – more from disappointment than pain – as the aggressor picked the knife back up and lunged at him. This time it went all the way, piercing the lad's stomach and, as he turned to shield himself, his back. The fierce man went on in a bloody frenzy as Anthony dropped down in a pool of his own blood – stabbing, slashing, slitting whatever portion of body came forth as his victim sort of slopped about in a sloshy mess.

The two onlookers just stood watching, aghast at the dreadful carnage presently unfolding before their own eyes. Neither seemed too shocked nor surprised, just worried – worried about themselves. Darren ended his onslaught by pulling Anthony's head up by his hair and dragging the knife across his throat. Coughing and spluttering, his head remained up as blood spurted all over the place. The slayer, soaked through, threw the weapon aside and stepped back; only now did he begin to let what he'd just done run through his mind. All at once he felt a squeezing in the pit of his stomach. Tighter, tighter. What had he done? In a way he felt that this was something that was always going to happen – it was written in stone, destined to occur just as he believed The Space coming to The Great Collective was always going to happen. This thought alone allowed Darren to immediately remove himself from any notion of responsibility, let alone blame and incrimination. He'd simply carried out an action that was always going to occur. If anything, Darren was the victim – or, at least, his mind was able to reach that conclusion. To not have done this to Anthony would have been fighting *against* The Space.

Still Anthony's head stayed up as the three men encircled him, growing more and more interested in studying the scene rather than recoiling in horror from it. He outstretched his hand once more towards Darren, who held out his own dripping hands and stared down at them.

Anthony's soaking mouth moved about, as if to try and speak for the first time in his life. No sound came out, but he kept doing it. The three men leant in to hear what he was trying to say. Nothing. The only sound from the apparently dying man was a wheezing release of air from the gaping slit in his neck, which neither worsened nor ceased as the men wondered what to do.

'He lives, he continues to exist,' Jim pointed out in a bizarre tone somewhere between mild surprise and awe.

'It is yet early to judge conclusively from our test,' Darren mused.

'No man can live through such a draining of blood,' Stephen cut in, his own breathing beginning to wheeze as the realisation of witnessing an attempted murder began to sink in. Darren had undertaken it with such ease, and it could easily have been himself lying on the ground in agony right now. He ran his fingers along his own neck as his sight lay fixed on Anthony's slit. 'We must help him, ease his suffering if he is to live.'

The gushing of blood had halted, and Anthony was making attempts at standing. Stephen gave him his hand, but he wouldn't take it; he reached out to Darren, who helped him to his feet.

'Remarkable,' Jim uttered, rubbing at his twitching eye. An intense spasm befell his face again and he cleared his throat and shook his head to try and stop it. His attention focused on the dead body of Peter, still lying where it fell. 'Utterly monstrous,' he carried on, his words powerful but his tone of voice devoid of feeling.

* * *

Peter Smith was dead, yet he was still experiencing consciousness. His location was nothingness and at the same time it existed – he was there, waiting. He knew he was waiting for something but didn't know what, and had no notion of the passage of time. Seconds, centuries; it was all the same here. None of it mattered. His entire being was up ahead spinning – a vast, or possibly minuscule, flat disc with no corners or sides besides the surface itself, pivoted in the centre by a flimsy dead stick that was endlessly there and yet on the brink of snapping. Peter reached out to himself and slammed his hand onto the wheel as he tried desperately to stop its incessant spinning. It would not cease and instead took Peter with it, his hand first sticking to and then being absorbed by the hazy surface. There seemed more beyond this flatness, some kind of depth, but it was beyond reach; the shallow material of the disc would not let up and allow more absorption other than the hand. As it carried him around and around and around, he flicked his vision from one area to another in a hopeless bid for either foresight or insight – looking, looking, looking, looking, looking.

1738

The simple washerwoman hurriedly made her way across the field, back towards her humble home. Hurry she did, but with a hint of a hobble as a lifetime of labour had left its toll on her round frame. She lived alone in a small shack of a thing where she did all her work for her wealthy clients. Right now she clutched tightly onto a swelling bundle of filthy clothes with her swollen knuckles, ready for a late night wash. The wealthy could be mucky folk. This latest load was extra work, on top of her hours and hours of daily work – it would all help pay her way. Her husband was dead, her children were dead. The desire to live still burnt brightly in her. She dreamt of past hardships replaced with future comforts and someone doing *her* washing. In her mind, she would achieve greatness too. It was just around the corner, just another step away.

She took another step forward, nearer her home and hopefully nearer to an easier life. As she did so, a huge sword swept across the darkness and took her head clean off. Her body and the dirty laundry dropped one way as her head plopped into a puddle the other way. A figure stepped forward, sticking the tip of the sword in the ground and brandishing a dagger. A foot kicked the washer woman's head aside and it bounced down the field, cushioned only by curly grey hair, as the murderer bent over the body and used the dagger to cut the hands off.

* * *

'There have been a number of mysterious deaths recorded here in Myrtleville which cannot possibly be attributed to a resurgence of the plague or any other pestilence,' the righteous Stephen Noble pointed out. Darren's eyes darted around the room mischievously. They came across Peter and he grinned at the sweating man. 'All the deceased are women of advancing years, and all have had various body parts removed. In each case, the woman has had her head lopped clean off. If we piece these missing parts together, we could almost make an entirely new woman – is this the intention of the slayer?

'What about the heads?' Darren asked.

'All have been found near the discarded bodies,' Stephen answered. 'One of the deaths is the wealthy landowner Thaddeus Hobble's wife Mimsie,' Stephen continued. 'A healthy reward has been offered by Hobble for the successful capture of her murderer… and the return of her breasts.'

'We could just pick up a homeless pauper and frame him for these murders to get our hands on the reward,' Jim offered, his eye twitching as he cleared his throat.

'We must use our connection to The Space for good,' Peter spoke up. 'This is our chance to start doing so. With a tiny bit of effort, we can solve this crime using our skills. For too long we have sat around and called ourselves The Great Collective, without doing anything great.'

'Why must we waste our time on this silly, trivial nonsense? We should be training our minds to strengthen our powers and seize control of the world,' Darren cut in.

'I balk at you, Aubrey!' Peter interjected. 'The man who hath used his connection to The Space to steal an apple off a child.'

'No such thing ever occurred!'

'We can set humanity on the right course,' Peter insisted.

'A course of our choosing, with us central to it,' Darren suggested. 'Your ideas appear to be shifting away from the general consensus, Peter,' he noticed. 'You are also struggling to remember the entirety of your prior existences.'

'Maybe that is a good thing. I feel this is somewhat of a curse.'

'We all remember the untold evils committed against us by our fellow man in lives gone by. No, we are above other men – we are The Great Collective.' Some of the gathering cheered, others mumbled their general support. 'You are thirty-six now, Peter,' Darren carried on, 'you have very little time left of this current life of yours.'

'I eagerly await a time when your allotted years cease before mine,' was Peter's cold fire back.

'There is some character in the bore, after all,' Darren chuckled. 'Tell me, Peter – would you rather spend your final few days clamouring to get your hands on Hobble's money only to never spend it, or would you go out in a bang of glory by committing a string of murders yourself on the enemies you have made in this life and go unpunished due to your imminent demise thereafter?'

'If I could remove *you*, I would,' Peter snapped at Darren. This prompted a mere grin from the receiver of this retaliation. 'I will persevere even harder to forget you in my next existence.'

'Forgetting me weakens your connection to The Space. Only with your mind fully immersed in Its grasp can you hope to retain and build upon your prior lives. You must reap what you have sown.'

Peter felt a sharp shiver ride down his spine as he fought hard to remove his mind from Darren's. Therein lay something in the corner; something shaded and altogether malevolent. It appeared as a tumour of mentality instead of physicality, hiding in its special little place away from dutiful eyes. Peter could see it as clear as night – as clearly as something in the darkness *can* be seen.

'Peter,' Stephen interrupted the pair, 'whether you like it or not, Darren is right. We are a collective – we move together. Move forward with us.'

'Darren does not move with us, he moves only for himself,' was Peter's response. All at once the tumour left Darren's mind and threw itself at his own. He looked around and could see it everywhere and nowhere. Everyone was afflicted one second and cured the next.

'We are here, together, for eternity. We are all icons, stuck with each other whether we like it or not,' Stephen went on. 'If you break away, if you weaken your link to The Space by watering down your memories, we shall all suffer. The Space came to us as a collective, not a singular. Stand with us, let us all agree on the actions we must take in the world and put them into action. We are all forgetting – the collective is beginning to dilute and splinter. Anthony is but one casualty of a much wider weakening.'

'You make a sensible case, Stephen, and this mystery with the incentive of Hobble's reward is enticing, but you still fail to see what I see,' Peter replied.

'We, as a collective, surely see all the same?' Jim came in.

'He claims to see that which we cannot,' Darren laughed, 'he thinks he stands apart from us and sees further than we can.'

'Praytell, do you see that which we do not?' Stephen asked as the rumblings from the gathering around them started getting more raucous.

'We have all experienced inherent evil in our lives, yet I am the only one who can see that it is infiltrating *us*. Surely we must use our position to stamp it out, not nurture it?' was Peter's reply.

'Preposterous,' Darren dismissed.

'Preposterous that there is evil within us, or that we must stamp it out?'

'We are finished here,' Darren concluded, rising to his feet. 'There is nothing more to be said today, only that you, Peter, should try to enjoy your final few days of this life.' Peter squinted across at him, his fists clenched. 'If my calculations are correct, you have less than a week to go.'

'Your attempt at calculation is a failure – I have nine days left.'

* * *

'You are hoping to stave off the dilution with that?' Stephen questioned Peter as they stepped up to Hobble's abode. Peter, having been scribbling away furiously in a notebook, pocketed it and grimaced at Stephen.

'If I could forget, I would,' was his grave response.

'But why? We can do whatever we so wish with our place in this world.'

'Yet we do not – we choose to tickle around and make drunkards hand us their last coins and other pointless trivialities. No, Stephen, I can see terrible evils coming. The Space reveals unimaginable horrors to me.'

'Such as?'

'Countless murder after murder, wicked sin after sin,' Peter sighed.

'Can you not be more specific?'

'Does The Space not show you?'

'I see what I wish to see – not what I do not.'

'Then you must keep it that way – no being would want to see what I have seen. There is untold darkness to come for the human race. A mere two hundred years from now, for example, millions will die by one man.'

'How can one man kill millions all by himself?'

'By controlling and influencing others. The Space even gives me a name – he will be called Hitler. I have made notes, I will make it my goal to stop him before he starts with his wickedness.' Peter tapped the pocket where he'd just placed his trusty notebook.

The pair looked up at the house before them – vast, endless in height and so very cold. The wind blew strong, slapping them with a severe, albeit brief, chill. Pale stones bled lazily into each other to make the walls, as rusty brown bars hid the windows. The men held their nerve as images flashed through their minds, images of a blood-stained corpse lying strewn in the woody grounds behind the building. The Space was showing them – when they stretched their minds in that direction, of course. Peter took hold of the brass knocker on the door and thrashed it three times. Soon it opened, a young woman stepping aside to let the men enter. Her deep brown eyes kept their gaze away from the new presence in her hall as she fumbled to keep her long dark hair under control in the rushing wind. She slammed the door shut and shot away before having a single word uttered to her. Peter and Stephen glanced at each other, before their sight fell once again on the mystery beauty exiting the room.

'She is a fine looking woman,' Stephen uttered.

'I didn't like her dress, it was a sickly green,' Peter replied.

'You don't need to like her dress... tis what lies *under* the dress that should interest you.'

'I cannot see what is under the dress.'

'Stretch your mind, my friend,' Stephen trilled, 'The Space allows many pleasures.' He winked at his cohort, who immediately felt uneasy. The Great Collective? They were surely destined to greater things than these kinds of seedy actions. Stephen could see Peter was displeased. 'You are a stranger with the women, Peter – you never allow yourself the base joys of the human body.'

'Perhaps I am saving myself for the right woman, or perhaps I cannot allow myself to grow close to a woman because I know I will die at thirty-six.'

Stephen laughed. 'That does not halt your ability to enjoy dalliances here and there. I, too, am like you in many ways but...' he trailed off, looking away at images etched into his mind from prior lives.

'Go on,' Peter encouraged, half-knowing what was coming.

'There is a woman, one woman, who keeps me from committing in the here and now. She comes to me, right at the end, just standing to deliver me to the next world. But no, I never get there – I am reborn and come back to life as Stephen Noble again in this world. She is a vision of perfection in all her intense golden hue. And, I know who she is.'

Peter, with some trepidation, asked: 'Who?'

'She is the *one*, the woman of my existence who waits for me in my final life. We shall be together at the end.'

'I see,' Peter whispered, turning from his friend. He thrust all his energy into sealing his mind right now, forcing a shell around himself as Stephen stood deep in thought. He wanted – had to – block any way of his mind being revealed to Stephen, because he too saw the same woman and *knew* that she would be with *him* and not Stephen in his final life. 'How do you know we will have a final life?' Peter eventually asked him.

'Even endlessness must cease in the end, surely?'

It seemed like there was a gust of wind carrying Thaddeus Hobble into the room – but no, it was just his thin legs. They danced as only thin legs could – quickly, and without order or method, as the lanky thing delivered himself to the men. 'Stephen Noble, Peter Smith – thank you for coming to me,' he said in a high yawn, holding out his hand. Before either man could stretch to shake it, Hobble had pulled it away and proceeded to wave it about the room. There was likely no reason for this other than to display and jig about the silk tassels dangling from his bright white sleeve. He was not a young man – far from it – but he was not aged. He wore the passage of time well on his taut face, and a thick head of white curls played well with the swooshing cloak draped over his narrow, slightly bent, shoulders.

'Honoured to meet the great Thaddeus Hobble,' Stephen cooed, bowing for added effect.

'At your service,' Peter joined in, nodding.

'You have met my daughter, gentlemen,' Hobble grinned furiously, lowering his head. 'Monetary reward is not all I offer you.'

'She is a fine looking specimen,' Stephen jumped, pushing Peter aside to get closer to the older man.

'Alas, poor Willemina – she cannot settle since her mother's murder. These are lawless times in which we live. The breasts she once suckled from as a babe are removed,' Hobble sighed. 'She needs a man to bring her from her stupor.'

'Indeed she does,' Darren replied grandly, appearing at the top of the stairs. Peter and Stephen were taken by surprise – Darren had clearly willed his presence here be kept secret from their roving minds.

'Ah,' Hobble joyously lapped, 'Master Aubrey.' It was now Hobble's turn to bow.

'What are you doing here?' Peter snapped.

'Exactly as I wish,' was his cryptic response as he slowly made his way down the stairs towards them. As he neared,

Hobble reached into his pocket and brought out a silk coin purse, dropping to his knees and outstretching his hand. Darren snatched it off him, slipping it into his own pocket. 'Payment number one,' he clarified.

'I feel ever so glorious!' Hobble elated, staying on his knees.

'I have planted that emotion within him,' Darren proclaimed in pleasure, 'for a small fee.'

'This is barbaric,' Peter barked.

'Nonsense! His wife hath been murdered, he had sunk into an irretrievable slump. I brought him back from that... I am The Curer.'

'You hast not brought the committer of his wife's murder to justice.'

'Tis immaterial.' Darren yawned, checking his pocket watch. 'Oh Peter, you are such a bore.'

'Better to be a bore than a petty crook,' Peter snapped back.

'Is it? Is it really?' Darren mused, half rhetorically, as he strolled away tapping his chin. This broke Hobble from his grip, and he got back on his feet.

'Come, my men, and I shall show you where Mimsie's murder occurred,' he said to them excitedly, as if the incident with Darren had never happened.

As they made their way towards the exit, Peter's attention was drawn to a minuscule brownish stain on the stone floor. There lay a door to one side, and vague images of a bloodied figure first emerging from it and then scrubbing furiously at the floor with a moist rag briefly flashed through his mind.

The vast garden to the rear of the property was just as Peter and Stephen had seen it in their vision; save for the dead body, which had now been removed and disposed of. Thick wisteria clung for dear life to a rotting pergola structure which separated the weedy stoned area from the mossy lawn beyond. Acres and acres of overgrown trees and hedging filled the rest of their view.

'And you say somebody emerged from the trees and just attacked your wife?' Stephen asked. It was now that Hobble's jovial demeanour soured.

'Oh Mimsie!' he sobbed, dashing to a patch of lawn and dropping to his knees in despair. He rubbed his hands on the moist grass, bringing his hands back to his face to sniff them. 'She was here, enjoying the fresh scent of our glorious natural world. I looked once and she was alive and happy, I looked again and she was strewn asunder with her beautiful thick neck cut clean in two.' He looked into the trees. 'I saw a figure shoot off in that direction carrying two sagging meaty lumps that were once her breasts, never to be seen again.'

'He went off in that direction, but he need not have necessarily come from that direction,' Stephen remarked.

'I did not see him arrive, no.'

'He may not be a he at all,' Peter thought out loud. 'This could be the work of a woman.'

'I am sure it was a man, though his features and clothing were ambiguous in the fractured haze.'

'Are you absolutely sure that he went off that way,' Peter questioned, pondering upon the stain inside, 'and not into the house?'

'Indeed. Tis I who darted in that direction to raise the alarm. I had my poor wife's blood all over my person after cradling her – it went everywhere.'

Peter could now see that the bloodied figure was indeed Hobble – he was weeping, whining about who could do this awful thing to his beloved. So distraught was he at the sight of his wife's innards now splashed haphazardly about the place – from his own hands, clothing and shoes – that he manically tore his shirt off and sought to polish them away with it.

'These murders plaguing Myrtleville,' Stephen sighed, 'always women of a certain age, always out in the open, and always some body part removed. They are wicked crimes.'

'Women are not safe to sit in their gardens, let alone walk the streets,' Hobble sniffled. 'I shall keep dear Willemina under lock and key from now on.'

'That would be a terrible shame for one so pretty,' Stephen chirped.

Hobble got up and rushed back to the men. 'Are you wealthy, my boy?' he asked Stephen with more than a hint of desperation.

'I may be, why?'

'If my daughter's hand is to be offered in marriage, then I must know it is not to a man so simply after the Hobble fortune.' He clasped Stephen's hand, and instantly there was the sense that the Hobble fortune was not as vast as was being made out. Stephen and Peter both eyed each other, having been delivered the same impression.

'The Hobble fortune,' Peter uttered, stroking the downy whiskers of his sideburns, 'I hear it hast diminished.'

'What?' Hobble sneered, pulling his hand from Stephen and pointing it at Peter. 'Where did you hear that from? Lies! Sheer lies!'

'We heard it from you,' Peter said with some glee.

'From your own mind,' Stephen added.

'But how?' Hobble fumbled, stumbling back. 'Sorcery!'

'By using our skills – skills which will aid in the capture of your wife's slayer,' Peter promised.

Hobble paced around, variously rubbing at his face and pulling at his baggy gown. Darren emerged from within the house and stood watch. 'You will be rewarded well if you can achieve such a feat,' Hobble committed, catching sight of Darren.

'I would like an official introduction to your delightful daughter Willemina, Mr Hobble,' Stephen asked.

'Of course, of course; come hence and it shall occur at once.'

The two men marched back into the house as Peter stepped onto the lawn and approached the scene of the crime. Darren lingered behind him as he closed his eyes and sniffed the air.

'What are you doing, you fool?' Darren laughed.

'I am reaching out to The Space for assistance in solving these murders.'

'Good luck with that,' Darren scoffed. 'Have you ever even asked yourself *why* The Space did what It did?'

'Why It gave us eternal life after life? Yes, I have. It is one of the only questions I cannot seem to be able to put to The Space.'

'You forget, Peter, you forget about that very first time It opened up to us – we never asked the where, why or how – we just went blindly into Its embrace.' Darren came closer to him… too close.

'What are you saying – I sense you do not trust The Space?'

'It aids us with ease in taking coin from Hobble, but struggles to bring up a suitable face for the crime committed against his wife.' Darren's face seemed to change, as though he was a new man entirely – not new, but so very different and afraid. 'It supports our endeavours toward ill, yet not our works of good.'

'It is not like that,' Peter yelled in frustration. 'Tis our own minds which are the evil, not The Space. What It reveals to us is a mere reflection of ourselves.'

'In that case, my drive for monetary gain is that much

more potent than your desire to put right that which is wrong,' Darren smirked, turning and strolling away.

He had a point. Peter stepped up to the house and sought out his reflection in the glass of a window – he felt then that he couldn't see himself. He was seeing a man that looked like him, yes, but not *him*. It was a difficult emotion to unravel and get to grips with... he was struggling to recognise this Peter Smith, a person he had been time and time again. The vivid memories were still there – Mother burning alive, The Space first allowing him to reach out to It – but he could no longer fully connect with them. He was an outsider, just looking in on someone else's lives. And yet, here he was *living* this life right now and staring at his genuine reflection. Darren's spin on their role in the world was tainted, and Peter now put his own current peculiar mood down to that.

* * *

Lock Lane Inn was a veritable feast of life at this time of an evening. That blindingly fierce ale would help even the most hardened cynic loosen their woes for a brief interlude of unabated merriment. This is exactly what Peter and Stephen now sought – simple, unashamed happiness. They moved briskly through the thick cloud of pipe smoke and landed at the bar, where a half-hunched bald man with a blister-covered face greeted them.

'Gentlemen,' he shouted above the racket in the room, pouring two pints of the only drink served in this place. Peter got his purse out to pay the man, but he shook his head. 'The money of a dead man is no good here.'

'What do you mean?' Peter asked, bemused, albeit quietly pleased at the free drinks. He was too tired to be on his game with The Space and try to peer inside the barman's mind for the answer.

'That Aubrey and his two minions were in here singing sad songs of your impending departure. A mere eight days left for dear Peter Smith.' He started crying, in a half-hearted sort of way, and didn't bother wiping away his tears. 'You will never know what it is to be old like me.'

Peter had lived thrice over, the first two times with only the same set of years. This third life was destined to end the same with just days to go. He never would learn the reality of old age – the privilege of singular longevity.

'Tis very sad,' Stephen consoled, putting his arm around Peter's shoulders as he brought his tankard to his lips. 'Very sad indeed.'

'I am not sad,' Peter replied stoically. 'I welcome inevitability – the end of this set of years. They haven't been the most interesting.' He grinned at the barman, who squinted back in confusion. 'I do hope I forget who I am next time around… I hope we all forget. At least that way there will be some respite from this drudgery.'

'He is delirious with his sickness,' the barman wept.

'Far from it – I have never been more focused in all my lives. And for now, I have the motivation of bringing to justice the murderer of these defenceless women.'

'Tis a plague on Myrtleville,' Stephen responded with sadness.

'Aye,' the barman cut in, 'or, as Lissy calls it, the culling.'

'The culling?' Peter questioned. 'Rather an odd way of putting it.'

'Almost like this Lissy thinks these murders a necessary occurrence,' Stephen added.

'This isn't old Eric Lissy, is it? Where can we find him this eve?'

'Him?' the barman laughed, which turned into a pained cough. 'You can find *Molly* Lissy right over there.' He pointed to the farthest point of the room, from where most of the frivolous noise was emanating, and stayed put to enjoy the impending scene.

'No, it can't be,' Peter gasped as he caught sight of a young woman standing on a table and swooshing her dress about. 'That's not Eric Lissy's little girl, is it?'

'Not so little any longer,' the barman chipped in, full of mirth. 'One of my best customers.'

Peter and Stephen briskly moved towards her, catching sight of her long bare legs as they danced about before their eyes.

'She is a delight to my vision,' Stephen uttered, taking in her long curly red hair and chubby freckled cheeks.

'I thought you were already taken with Willemina Hobble?'

'Tis advisable to keep your options open, my friend.'

Rather too distracted, Stephen now bumped into a particularly bulky man, knocking the drink from his hand. Stephen, still safely clasping his own drink, took a large gulp from it and smiled back as the big man froze in shock. His eyes, which had been so happily fixed on Molly as he and the other lecherous men had ogled her, slowly moved to look down on Stephen. Look down they did, for this beast of a creature stood a good foot taller than he. Stephen was not a small man by any means – far from it, in fact – it just so happened that this creature had been built with no height restrictions in place. Before he could react, Stephen had the man's bear claw around his neck and he was squeezing the life out of him. Confident he could not die before his time, neither Stephen nor Peter did anything about this attack. Angered at the removal of the attention from herself, Molly dropped her skirt and snatched a glass from another man's hand, which she brought crashing down on the hefty's head. Instantly he let go of Stephen and momentarily stumbled around in a daze, before his swelled frame came crashing down with an almighty thud. Overcome with some unearthly thrill, Molly roared as she jumped down off the table and landed on the unconscious man's back. She jumped up and down on him as the rest of her gathering goaded her on.

'Who are you two little weeds, then?' she shouted out to the new arrivals. Peter and Stephen looked at each other in dismay. Before they could answer, her feet came slamming onto the floor as they left the man's back, and she skipped off towards the bar. There, the barman poured her a drink, which she downed in one go. Rubbing her moist mouth, and shaking some spillage off her top, she turned to Peter and Stephen. 'What are you after, a good hiding like Davy over there? Some men enjoy a good spanking from a strong woman.' She leant in and winked.

'We're here about the murders,' Peter called back over the din. Suddenly, Molly's carefree demeanour soured. She stood there, rigid, staring intently back at the two men. Slamming her empty glass down on the bar, she growled. The barman filled it up again and it barely touched the sides of her mouth as she gulped it down.

'We hear you're calling these murders the culling,' Stephen added.

She grabbed the pair and dragged them across the Inn and out through the door. Before they knew it, they were in the ditch across the lane with Molly on top of them. 'Shh,' she whispered, placing a finger each to both man's lips. 'You can never be too careful who's listening in.'

'What do you mean?' Peter whispered back.

'There are wicked people all over Myrtleville – not one of us can drop our guard,' she said fearfully, getting closer to the men. They did not complain. Peter, in particular, felt his heart racing as her bosom pressed up against his own chest. He at that very moment wished Stephen was not with them – that he and Molly were alone and free to do as they wished… or as he wished. Alas, Stephen *was* there and he could read Peter like a book. Literally, for a simple stretch in the right direction gave him grace to leap right into Peter's mind and hear his thoughts.

'You are safe with us,' Stephen called out, rather too loudly, breaking the physical contact of the two and delivering more pressure from Molly's finger against his lips. 'Your hands are coarse for a girl your age,' he carried on, taking hold of them and rubbing the palms. 'They have seen much work, I would not impugn. Yet, they are equally as tender – I would have them explore my flesh at the drop of a hat.' His face creased as he eyed the young girl seedily. Peter rolled his eyes and felt a bit queasy. Still, he himself had only just had thoughts of that very nature regarding Molly.

'I am but 16 years of age, you old dog,' Molly snapped back, slapping Stephen across the face. 'You are old enough to be my father.'

'I am not yet 30!' Stephen gasped. 'Peter is older than I am,' he hastened to add, noting the coy look the pair had just given each other.

'I may appear forthcoming, but that is just my nature. I am not to be *had* by any man, least of all either of you wrinkled old toads,' she finished.

'Very well,' Peter responded with some sadness, 'not that that is the intention of either of us. No, we are at you to dig deeper into the mystery of these murders.'

'Why do you call them the culling?' Stephen iterated.

'That is simply what I overheard at the Aubrey residence.'

'Aubrey residence?!'

'Yes – I am employed as a handy girl. I can put my hand to any task calling.'

Stephen and Peter didn't need to look at each other or utter a single word to know what the other was now thinking – Darren Aubrey had turned to murder. They both jumped the gun, conjuring up images in their minds that showed Darren actually doing the deeds. Were these to prove to be real or imagined would be the next discovery that these intrepid investigators were hoping to uncover.

* * *

Peter jotted something in his notebook, swiftly pocketing it as Stephen attempted a glimpse at its contents.

'You may well be a fool scribing all of these happenings,' Stephen mused, half seeing the secrets within those pages via The Space's help. 'They could fall into the wrong hands.'

Peter raised an eyebrow, thinking it unwise to do anything else. In fact, most of his energy was being used up trying to keep his mental wall up to deter prying from Stephen and others into his mind. It was becoming exhausting. The pair crouched down behind some shrubs outside Aubrey Manor – a rather grand title for a building which equated to far less than Hobble's abode. Nevertheless, Darren had managed to achieve minor wealth and enjoyed a relative life of comfort and ease due to activities likely enhanced by his connection to The Space. The man himself looked on from a small window in the roof, knowing full well what Peter and Stephen were up to. Next to him stood Anthony the silent, his bottom lip gaped and moist. His bulky arms lay clumsily by his sides as he stared vacantly at the inclined wall of this attic room. Darren clicked his fingers at the encroaching, yet dormant, giant and immediately Anthony turned to face him.

'They are here, Tony – they have come to disrupt our enjoyment of things.'

Anthony frowned, which made Darren smirk all the more. He turned momentarily from Anthony to gaze upon a portrait of a brightly coloured parrot. Its beak open, and mirth and merriment writ upon the rest of the feathered face, Darren couldn't help but pet the image with a pat and a chin tickle. Anthony did not watch, instead focussing on anything and nothing. Perhaps he saw more than anyone else did – perhaps he saw nothing at all.

At that moment Molly walked in with a moist brown rag and proceeded to swing it loosely about the cobwebbed room.

'What are you doing in here, girl?' Darren snapped, his attention taken from both the parrot portrait and the men outside in the shrubbery.

'Cleaning,' she responded joyously, a twinkle in her eye.

'Tis not needed here, the dust helps preserve my painting – move along and spruce other areas of my building.' He tapped his chin, adding: 'Prepare a cold meal for Anthony… his concentration is beginning to slacken.' Molly huffed and departed, the door closing behind her.

'Petulant thing,' Darren sulked, turning once again to look down on Peter and Stephen. They were gone. 'Living off seeds,' Darren pondered, turning back to the parrot portrait, 'what an existence.' Now he thought about Peter Smith, and he felt overwhelmed with loss. 'He judges me,' he told the portrait, 'he stands in judgement over me, yet The Space came to me also. Peter is as righteous as the rest of us – oh indeed!' He turned towards Anthony, to find the silent one had moved closer to him. 'You are loyal no matter what miseries I wage upon you,' he said of the bigger man. 'I see many miseries waged both upon and by me – are the two kinds any different?' There was no answer from Anthony save for a vacant stare. 'Pity.'

* * *

Peter and Stephen had reached the building and were scurrying along it. The former was leading and pushed a huge thick bramble out of his way, which sprung back and caught the latter right across the face.

'Careful,' Stephen winced as he pulled the thorny growth from his skin. Peter kept on moving forward. 'Count yourself lucky you are to die in a few days,' he mumbled under his breath.

As he looked up ahead at Peter moving steadily along, his mind filled with the plain woman. It was as though both men were not actually attempting to gain access to Darren's house at all, but were instead in competition to reach her. He saw her just beyond Peter – who was nearer than he – and he quickened his pace, feeling he should have the lead and not his competitor. Faster he moved, desperation taking hold as he sensed Peter holding the advantage. It was not really to his true advantage, however, as his face was the first to meet with the huge log that Anthony swung at them from around the corner of the house. The Space had not warned them, and Stephen was not quick enough to react; he too went tumbling to the ground upon finding his face smashed with the heavy rough object. Darren appeared from behind his man to survey the carnage as Anthony lifted the log into the air, ready to bring it crashing down again upon the men. His master gently eased it down.

'No, not yet – first we bring them inside,' he whispered joyously to the silent one. 'I have made plans.'

* * *

'The culling is a necessity, though I am not the perpetrator,' Darren explained as Peter and Stephen lay flat out on stone beds. Their arms were secured above their heads and their legs below, stretched out as tightly as Anthony could manage to pull. He now stood and watched from a distance in the dark stone-walled room as Darren waxed lyrical. 'The deaths illuminate a very salient point of mine – The Space aides us only in bad.' He stepped up to Peter, poking his finger into one of the bloody gashes on his face. Peter cried in agony. 'Not one accurate vision of the murders has been delivered to any of The Great Collective, nor indeed was a vision of the impending smashing of your faces. Bad is good.'

'No, lies,' Peter yelled out, twisting his body as he tried desperately to free himself.

'He's right, Peter,' Stephen whimpered, overcome with pain and apparent epiphany. Darren roared with joy.

'The identity of the murderer isn't at all important here, it is the demonstration of The Space's preferences that we must focus on.'

'It is a reflection of us,' Peter tried to argue.

Stephen began to weep. 'You are truly right, Aubrey. Truly, truly,' he sobbed.

Darren nodded to Anthony, who came over and loosened Stephen's bonds. The pair helped him off the stone slab and eased him onto his feet. 'You will join us, the new Great Collective – controllers of humanity's destiny.'

Stephen nodded in agreement.

'No, no, NO,' Peter kept on.

'Oh do be quiet. Tis a shame, you have a superb mind when pointed in the correct direction,' Darren cooed. 'You have what, six, seven days left to live? You will live them down here in my dungeon, bound and starved. I trust you shall suffer… with any luck.'

The threesome made their exit, sealing the door shut and leaving Peter to his fate. He lay there, stretching his mind toward The Space, wondering whether it best he indeed just stay down here to rot. He had suffered before, and would suffer again – there was nothing he couldn't handle. In a way he felt quite pleased that Darren had removed him from the outside world to perish down here. It saved him having to do anything else.

The Space was at once with him, he knew it. He saw everything that ever was, is or will be rushing through his mind – the overbearing completeness crushing him down like an avalanche. It was all too much to comprehend, all too much to try and pick out what he wanted to know. It dawned on him that he didn't *want* to know anything – he wanted to die right there and then and never return. What he had witnessed so far in his lives was enough to set him wholly against this 'gift' from The Space. The good was drowned out by all the evil, which far outweighed its counterpart – even the good, Peter now saw as a tiny step away from cruelty. He was completely resigned, completely accepting of the total extinction of himself.

From out of the shadows emerged a true guardian angel, the abundance of curly golden reddish hair falling about as she struggled to undo the binds Anthony had tied. It was Molly, come to rescue him. Peter wanted to feel devastation at this easy escape, but he couldn't help feeling some kind of appreciation for Molly for risking her own neck to do it. He now pushed The Space away in an attempt to block any intrusion from Darren into what was occurring. He could escape, he could solve the murders… he could make a life with Molly. No. He had just a week to live. He could make nothing whatsoever with Molly, or anyone else for that matter, and it was this that hurt him the most. There was the plain blonde woman – she would save him. Molly, who was currently saving him, helped him to his feet.

'Your face looks a sorry sight,' she remarked, unable to take her piercing blue eyes off it.

'Thank you.'

'What now?' Molly wondered, aiding Peter's pained steps toward the door.

'We inform Hobble that we have found our murderer.'

'Master Aubrey? But, I heard, he says he was not responsible.'

'That may be, but you can collect the reward and we can cause some trouble for Darren,' Peter chuckled through gritted teeth. 'You will be your own kept woman with the money.'

'And what about you, you will surely want some coin?'

'Not I.'

Molly looked distrustingly at him. 'What about doing the right thing? The real murderer will remain at large.'

'Maybe Darren did commit them, perhaps he is lying?'

She moved from Peter ever so slightly. 'You have changed.'

'I am seeing more clearly now,' was his quick response.

'You are seeing what you want to see, not what you should see.'

Peter narrowed his eyes, responding with: 'You are saying what you think you should say, not what you-'

'Do *not* speak to me like that,' Molly snapped back.

'You are but a girl, I shall speak to you as I see fit,' Peter roared back, growing annoyed by this canon in front of him.

She slapped him sharply, which sent him tumbling to the floor. There he cried, unable to stop himself though not knowing why.

'Now look what you made me do,' she huffed, folding her arms to keep them from doing any more damage.

'You are so beautiful,' was the lump of flesh's sad reply.

'And you are ugly,' she shot back. Peter looked rather accepting of and agreeable to this. Molly suddenly felt she had been a bit harsh. Yes, she did not find him attractive, but to hurt the man at such a weak moment for him wasn't the nicest thing to do. 'Is my physical state the only thing that sets me apart from any others your sight may fall upon?'

'I do try to see beyond the mere physical,' Peter flubbed, clearing his tears. 'Such a thing is a difficult task for men.'

'And for women,' Molly added.

'Then, perhaps, we are on an equal footing?'

'We are not equal,' she laughed, sticking her hand out towards him. At first he flinched, but eventually accepted her aid and got back on his feet with her help. 'We shall go and see Hobble, but only to warn him about Aubrey and not accuse him.'

Peter nodded.

* * *

'You come here to warn me about Aubrey, yet fail to deliver the name of my wife's slayer?' Hobble flounced as Peter and Molly stood in his doorway. 'I am both perplexed and intrigued, and remain ill at ease as a brutal beheader remains at large.' His eyes flitted back and to into the distance above their heads. He stood aside and beckoned them inside. There, at the foot of the grand staircase, stood Willemina with her back to the guests. Her silence seemed deafening to Peter, and her stillness like a mountain top crashing into a valley below. He could not understand this piercing siren and had no time to dwell on her further as Hobble swept them into a side room.

Before he knew it, Peter found himself slouched in a

ruby red chair with a glass of wine in his hand. 'Tis the finest wine to ever pass my lips – do you feel honoured to be given it freely?' Hobble questioned, hovering over him.

'Nothing is ever free,' Peter pondered under his breath, taking a sip. It did taste pleasant enough but nothing special. His eyes slid across the room to where Molly was seated. Hobble was suddenly now next to her – Peter had not seen him move. He poured the liquid into her glass and turned to smile at Peter.

'You think me a foolish man to trust in Darren Aubrey?'

'He is a wicked man, bent on wrongdoing of the highest order,' Molly answered, before Peter could even open his lips.

'Yet you say he is not the murderer?' Hobble again asked Peter, a brief flicker in his eyes directed down at Molly. Peter cleared his throat, sitting up somewhat. 'One is of course overjoyed at your warning of the aforementioned rat,' Hobble carried on just as his male guest tried to speak. He slowly slinked across the room to Peter, undoing his red velvet waistcoat. Out flopped a coin purse on a string and the seated one watched as it dangled in front of him. 'Your reward.'

'That is of no use to me,' Peter responded, his hand instinctively stretching out to take it. In an instant the sight of his own outstretched hand became blurred. 'Give it to the girl.'

'I fully intend to,' was Hobble's reply as he pocketed the purse and smiled.

Peter saw the glass slip out of his own hand as his entire body went numb. His heavy eyes looked at Hobble – he'd given his guests a drink, but hadn't had one himself.

* * *

49

'Your jottings fascinate me,' Hobble uttered as Peter lifted his head up. At first he saw the older man flicking through his notebook, then behind him some ghastly headless body hanging from a hook attached to the exposed neck. Seams ran all across it, a mishmash of skin and parts from umpteen women stuck together to make up this dreadful yellowy blue carcass. He looked around the darkened room, but could not see Molly.

'Where is Molly?' Peter demanded, struggling to free himself from weighty chains.

'The Space sounds so wondrous – and immortality, what an honour,' he carried on, waving the notebook about, ignoring the captive's question. 'I do believe I have lured in and captured the correct candidate.'

'Candidate?'

'The perfect female body,' Hobble insisted, pocketing the notebook and stepping over to the sagging meat and flesh, 'but with a male brain – *your* brain, Peter. I set up the reward in order to lure the cleverest here in order to harvest their brain for my experiment – if they were clever enough to work out the truth, they would make the ideal candidate.'

'But I didn't work out the truth, I thought Darren did it,' Peter gulped, his mind now full of ghastly images of Hobble committing the crimes. The Space was a little too late on that one.

'Immaterial – your writings are enough to convince me of your superior brain.'

'Thanks,' Peter mused, 'I think… So, my head and a woman's body?'

'No, no, just your brain. I already have a head, a fresh one too,' he grinned as he bent down and reached into a bucket full of reddened water, lifting out Molly's severed head by her lovely long wet hair. The most agonising pain hit Peter's chest, plunging into the pit of his stomach like a fireball hitting Earth's surface from outer space. 'She has a beautiful face,' Hobble continued, lifting the head higher and swinging it so that the face faced him. 'It will take a careful cut at the back of her head to remove her brain and replace it with yours so as not to damage this face. Tis the face of my future wife.'

'What about the wife whose breasts you removed?' Peter sighed to himself, all of humanity now a sick perversion in his eyes, as he looked over at the headless body hanging there. The dark yellow breasts were big, but sagged and hung there in sullen depression. He didn't know whether it was the angle he was positioned at or not, but from where he was looking they seemed to have been attached in an unbalanced fashion. The left one had been sewn on far higher than the right.

Hobble, meanwhile, had dumped Molly's head back in the bucket and was caressing the body's nipples. 'Her breasts were stupendous – the rest of her horrendous,' he trilled. 'I kept her best bits, and got rid of the rest.'

Right then a side door opened, and in walked Willemina. Silently she floated up to Peter, her sad brown eyes looking him up and down. Her mouth creased as she reached out and placed a hand on his chest, some flicker of emotion he could not read playing on her spotty face.

'Your father is a cruel murderer of umpteen women,' Peter pleaded, 'only you can stop him.'

She looked up at his lips as they moved, but didn't seem to register the words bursting forth.

'Futile, my friend,' Hobble called from across the room, 'although my daughter *is* taken with you.'

'I sense an unused body,' she suddenly said in a deep whisper. 'All human desire held back and wasted…' her hand rubbed at Peter's chest, moving up to his throat, 'or put aside and saved for the right woman.' Her boney pink fingers came to rest on Peter's face as she caressed his sunken cheek. 'Father,' she let go of Peter and turned to Hobble, 'I want to keep this one as my husband.'

'Very well, you may keep his body; but I require his brain.'

'Tis the brain I wish to possess more than anything else of his,' she called back. Hobble did not look pleased. 'Father, I think it a little peculiar that you wish my new mother to have a male brain.' She folded her arms and smirked. Peter just stayed fixed behind them, withdrawn and aghast at these weirdos.

'A man's brain is far superior to a woman's, my dear,' he said softly as though speaking to a child, coming to her and placing an arm across her shoulders.

Willemina's face scrunched up as she gritted her teeth, but she did not vocally disagree with her father. Instead, she wriggled out of his clutches and turned back to Peter. Hobble grinned with apparent victory and moved back over to his new wife, taking the bucket with Molly's head in with him. His back now turned to the pair, he lifted off his sword from a hook on the wall and pulled a cloth off a large stone. He made himself busy sharpening his weapon as Willemina stared intently into Peter's eyes. He looked back, at first seeing nothing but warm brown eyes that felt icy and evil. As he continued, and time seemed to freeze, she in turn did become warm and full of something Peter couldn't quite get to. He briefly flicked his eyes over to Hobble, whose movements had frozen in a mist and appeared much further away now.

He thought about Darren using The Space for his own ends, and now threw his mind into Willemina's. She stood still, as before, looking back at the man she wanted as her husband. Her mind was sectioned in ceaseless layer upon layer of conflicting behaviours and motives, but, her hopes and desires were singular and focused in one area – the want and need for love and acceptance from her father, and the willingness to do anything to maintain that. And yet, there now came a new spark, one which Peter knew instantly represented himself. There stood the two opposing sides, one for Father and one for the new man in her life, the merest of space still just separating the two. Father's side had advanced, ready to quash Peter's. It was up to the latter to arm his own in her mind and destroy the opposition. He pulled from her mind, put aside The Space and realised he could do this alone.

'I am your future,' he whispered to her. She leant closer, their faces almost touching. 'I will be the new man in your life. I love you.'

She kissed him and he reciprocated, wishing he could reach out were his body not bound. Suddenly her hands reached around to the lock keeping his chains fixed. She pulled a key from her pocket and winked, sticking it in the lock. Before she could turn it, her head shot away and Peter found himself covered in blood as it squirted from her exposed neck. Behind her, with his sword, stood Hobble. He put the weapon down and went across to pick up his daughter's head as her body dropped against Peter. He pulled back as much as he could and it slid down between his legs, slumping half on the floor and half on him. The blood kept pouring out in his lap as Hobble placed the head on top of his new wife.

'Why did I not think of this before? My own daughter – beautiful *and* with the necessary intelligence to keep her brain intact.' He kicked the bucket with Molly's head in aside, and it tipped over and spilt out across the floor. The head came to rest upright, the features looking pained and frustrated. 'You are no longer required, Peter Smith,'

Hobble sighed in relief as he stayed fixed in wonderment at his completed invention.

* * *

Peter had no idea how little or how long had passed in time down here – he simply knew that his own life was about to come to a close. Not by Hobble, but by the curse of The Space's gift. It could be yet another day or two, or it could seconds. He'd lost track, but he didn't care. He was ready to leave this time and this place and hopefully never come back to humanity. But, he knew that simply wouldn't be the case. He'd be reborn again in a future that brought yet more pain and hardship. If only to forget what had gone before in past lives would be a gift – to never remember The Great Collective and The Space would at least aid in some form of quiet normality.

Up ahead, Hobble busied himself putting the finishing touches to his new wife – she now had a head, and was no longer hung up. She lay flat out on a wooden bed which Peter had witnessed Hobble construct; now and again, as her "husband" mopped her brow or checked for a pulse, a bit of skin would flap open or a finger would fall off. The manufacturer of this thing was quick to repair the fault, and so it went on. Luckily it was cold in here, but decay had certainly been occurring – Peter could smell it. Flies occasionally buzzed around when Hobble left the door open for any length of time (which wasn't often), but apart from that fresh air didn't seem to want to come in here. Nothing would want to come in here.

'Use The Space,' Hobble suddenly cried, waving Peter's notebook in his face, 'bring her to life with your magic.' Peter simply didn't respond.

As Hobble lay down in bed next to his creation, the big

upright box appeared and obscured Peter's view of them. With It came the thin, plain woman. Her blonde hair hung over her face, hiding any features which Peter may have recognised. He thought back to the first time he'd seen her – he'd called out, asking who she was. He knew even less about her this time, yet she was perfection in his mind. She was patiently waiting for him in the future, ready to give him the life he so desperately wanted. Then, the image of Stephen appeared by her side and took her hand, smiling at Peter as he felt the heavy pulse of death rush through him. He slumped in his chains, down in Hobble's dungeon, dead.

* * *

'We are The Great Collective, we are the controllers of humanity's destiny,' Darren addressed the gathering in their meeting hall deep beneath Myrtle Forest. Amongst the group stood Stephen, Jim and Anthony. 'If we work together we can utterly dominate the entire world.' A roar of jubilation and agreement reverberated around the room, shaking its very stability – clumps of the earthen walls plummeted down around them as the cheering continued. There was no conscience, no Peter Smith, to stop them now.

PART TWO

SEPARATED BEFORE BIRTH

The fact is that once you get watered down, you forget yourself. And, if you keep on repeating your life in ascending existences, it becomes increasingly difficult to remember all that has gone before. You are quite quickly wrapped up in the here and now, living and being about the current set of years. For The Great Collective, that came about when they got watered down and forgot themselves. They could not stay fixed as a united unit, instead being torn apart by the horrors they both witnessed and were a part of. It was simply better to push away all that was terrible about humanity and hide away. That they did, but the residual memories of their past lives and the unending recurrence thereafter of more existences would be inescapable. Separated before birth, they lived out their lives without the previous knowledge they had been so overwhelmed with. But, it was always there... somewhere.

STEPHEN'S UNFORTUNATE REMOVAL

I am a difficult person. I am afforded good looks, which gets me the attention of many a female – equally, I am disfigured inside where no woman, or even medical person, could see. My troubling nature has landed me on this ship as a fag of a slave, mopping up after the pompous 'higher' men and generally being a lackey. My family's own moderate wealth has at the very least delivered me on board a survey voyage and not some ghastly war effort. Perhaps that is a sadness, as I feel even less purpose aboard Beagle as I did ashore. I keep no check on our location, and take no interest in the survey itself – my only mental stimulation is the going over of my own thoughts. They are a sifting through of two main events in my life: the final straw that broke my family's patience and led to my presence here, and a recurring dream I have of a large upright box emanating a powerful force and a rather plain yet alluring blonde woman coming either from within it or alongside it. Both are, what you might call, a bloody bind. Let me tell you about how all this began – sit back and savour this wonderful recounting.

The two events, though separate, could be construed as linked. The latter – that of the woman and the box – ultimately resulted in the former – the final straw. No straw was actually broken, but to describe the breaking of something is getting somewhat near to what happened. Yes, the woman in my dream, let us begin there. As I say, from what my sleeping vision would allow me to see of her when I first saw her, she was at first glance rather plain. I have, in the past, judged very much on first looks – they can be a good indication of many things about a person; a rogue and a ruffian can be quickly picked from a gathering of otherwise educated and wealthy individuals. This plain woman – I could not ascertain her place in society at all. Her drab white garments merely allowed a bleeding of colour from her pale face and long, thin, blonde hair. I wanted to get to her, but could not. She was but a figment of my slumber. That is when I struck at the idea of tracking her down in the waking world – that was my only way of getting to her. To say I found her would be to mock both my wonderful dream and give credence to the person I thought was her. The woman I came across was very similar indeed to the one I'd envisaged and I set my sights on her. What followed, of course, will be of interest to the men who say they cannot form tears. Let me tell you, men can cry – especially when their manhood is compromised.

There was absolutely no point making a play for Lauren. So many boys, and then young men, had tried and ultimately failed to succeed with her. She was having none of it – nothing whatsoever. Gossip was she'd never even allowed a boy to kiss her, let alone do anything else. She never lacked attention, either, in fact far from it. In her younger days there was a healthy queue of boys eagerly waiting to have their go at breaking her cold hard starvation of romance. But, no, none of them ever succeeded.

She was not the most beautiful of women, but she was not ugly either. Slim, almost unhealthily so, and rather pale with a pointed nose, her blonde hair remained tied up in a tight bun atop her head. Nobody ever saw her with her hair down – nobody ever saw anything more of her than what she wanted to show – her pale face, and her pink hands. The rest lay hidden beneath a small ever-circling collection of bland baggy white dresses. The fact she was so neglecting of her sexual nature was the key pull for all these men, including myself. Would I be the one to break through? The challenge was enticing. And, the mystery of what she was capable of in the bedroom was instantly alluring.

Eventually, of course, as the years went by – and they did, quickly – the interest men showed in her wained. One man whose interest in Lauren never abated was myself. I say man, but I was more a boy. I'd known her since I was a very little boy – she was already a woman by then. She had almost shown me affection… once. Our hands had brushed together when I was out playing with some other boys one summer's day. She was briskly making her way through the village, undertaking some business nobody else was privy to. She had paused, our eyes had met, and I had fallen head over heels in love. The years passed, of course, and I grew into the handsome devil I am now. Never did I give in to the affections of the women who flocked to my feet. No, I wanted the woman I had had visions of during slumber. It was not until a moment of epiphany that I realised they were one and the same – the woman from the box was Lauren. She *had* to be. However, I was puzzled – the woman in my dream had her face shielded by her hair, yet Lauren's face was clear to see. It was all that could be seen of Lauren's. I felt that I saw everything but the face of the one in my vision, so to place Lauren's there instead was the perfect solution. I now wanted her even more than before – she was all I thought about. All she thought about was… well, nobody knew. She had never let anyone in, never dropped the barricade she'd thrown up around herself.

I began to experience my dream more and more, until I

could envisage it every time my eyes sealed shut. I would think about that dratted cold woman every single day too during my waking hours. I had no release from this desperate situation I'd let myself spiral into. Lauren, too, seemed caught in a trap that I just couldn't see her breaking free from. The absolute only solution was my interference, nay, my help in her life. But, for all the outside world she just did not have the sexual urges that I did. No – to all intents and purposes she appeared completely asexual. This began to drive me mad, and I started setting out all kinds of plans. Firstly, I was going to construct a purpose-built dungeon in which to house Lauren as my sex slave, then I was simply going to pluck up the courage to just ask her for a courtship and see where things went. Eventually I decided upon breaking into her house and 'think on my feet' when there.

One night I did just that, dressing up in my best clothes and heading over to her house in the very early hours. Creeping around the back, I put my muscles against the door and forced it open. Utter silence hit my ears inside, and so I gingerly moved about in the darkness. All of a sudden, however, a heavy weight came crashing on the back of my head and I dived straight into the first silent sleep I'd had in a long time. No woman, no big box; just emptiness.

* * *

I wakened with a splitting headache. Keen I was to clutch it to in some way try and ease the pain, but it was no good – my hands were bound tightly above my head. I tried to rub my head between my arms, but quickly I grew tired and concentrated more on how sore my hands and arms were becoming. They were supporting my entire body, as my dead weight hung there supported by them. I felt cold and looked down to see that I was naked, my penis drooping like a new sausage slipping out of a butcher's hands. The room was dull and dreary, the faint smell of grease permeating from the cooking stove ahead of me. On top of it sat a filthy shallow pan. Suddenly, the door ahead opened and Lauren walked in, going over to the stove and lighting it. She moved the pan about, loosening the hard grease within as the heat from below melted it. I stayed silent, just watching in awe as she went about this basic task. Was this to be our first meal together as a loving couple?

Without a single word uttered between us, Lauren brought out a knife and stepped up to me. I looked at her – the first time I'd seen her this close in a long time – and felt utterly terrified. She took hold of my penis and slashed it clean off with the knife. I couldn't feel it, I was in complete shock, watching on as she tossed the severed object into the frying pan and cooked it. Blood bubbled and spat and my penis became all burnt and hard. When Lauren decided it was cooked enough, she removed the pan from the stove and pricked my cooked penis out with a fork. She marched back over to me, opened my mouth and forced it into it. The searing heat of it at once burnt the inside of my mouth, and then choked me as Lauren forced it further down my throat with the fork. She stepped back, smiling, as I writhed in agony and jerked my neck back and forth to try and dislodge the charred remains of my manhood. Blood poured out of the stump betwixt my legs and I felt no more air enter my lungs.

It was a few minutes more before Lauren's smile turned to a frown as she perhaps became upset at my lack of death. I too was puzzled why I had yet to succumb to this torture. She grabbed hold of the knife and buried it into my chest, leaving it there, as I again wriggled and writhed in pain. Still death did not come. My attacker began looking very stressed and overwhelmed with the situation, for the first time ever letting her hair down as she pulled at it. It hung completely over her face, concealing it, as she lunged forward and pulled the knife from my chest. Frantically she thrust at her own chest with the weapon, stabbing herself a dozen or more times as I carried on choking. Soon she fell in a heap, throwing the knife at me with her last ounce of strength and clutching at the wounds on her chest. She fell backwards, hitting her head on the stove and rolling forward onto her side. I stayed, hanging there, the choking a constant sensation for a week or more as Lauren's body rotted in front of me.

It was not until the stench of her decaying corpse, which had so filled my own nostrils for endless days, raised some villagers that I was freed. My body was completely drained of blood and the sorcery of my survival was quick to fill their minds. I was indeed lucky to survive – they sealed the stumpy wound that was once my penis with salt.

* * *

So here I am, on Beagle, with no penis. I think constantly of Lauren, the woman who I saw in my dreams and fell in love with only to watch her kill herself and turn to a maggot-eaten pile of stinky sludge. She was the never girl – the only penis she had ever touched was the one she'd quickly dashed off with a knife and cooked. In some ways that drew me closer to her; she had been able, right at the end of her life, to touch a naked man. I am that man, and it was worth losing my penis over.

To try and give my life meaning this far along is utterly pointless. I just repeat what I have done the previous day, and follow orders. My very brief moments of rest are used up, as I say, with thinking over my past. I say past, but it would feel more natural to say pasts. It sounds perfectly mad to surmise that I do not feel this has been or will be my only life. I have been unable to get to the bottom of the idea, but I do feel that I have been here, on this Earth, before – and will be again. I sense that I know things and have many other life experiences, but cannot completely remember. It is an aching sort of feeling. I am wholly alone in these thoughts, with not one single friendly shipmate to discuss them with. I have only briefly come close to making a friend, but I scuppered any burgeoning connection. Charles his name is; one of those geologists who think they see things that aren't immediately there. That's what initially drew me to him. Our first conversation, though on a subject which bored me, was nonetheless an enticing link back to my own niggle of an unreachable memory.

We had come ashore some peculiar island inhabited by weird creatures I had never seen before, and cared not to really look at. My mind was insular, my vision warped. 'All of these animals I have studied,' he called out to me as I passed, 'are both similar and different in equal measure.' I yawned, but stopped.

'What do you mean?'

'This giant tortoise,' he went on waving his hands at one, as though I should have known what he was trying to tell me.

'Big, isn't it,' I responded glibly.

'Very big, and yet I have seen other adult tortoises in other parts of the world which are minuscule in comparison.'

'And?' I pushed, tiring somewhat at his lack of clarity.

'Where the tortoises are small, the food is less and their predators more. Here, I see no natural predator and the food is abundant – both may have shared a common ancestor, yet have adapted to their surroundings.'

He trailed off, turning from me in excitement and darting away. I mused more on his motivations than what he'd actually said, likening his search for something to my own. My life here, right now, is on hold; shut off and without merit. I am travelling the world, but feel separate from it. Half the man. No, quarter the man. It is as though there is more of me out in the distance somewhere – both similar to me and just slightly different – not remembering who I have been or who I will become.

DARREN THE DANDELION
CHILD

It is difficult to appreciate one's own life until it has been endangered, or is undeniably coming to its end. For me, I have experienced both of these – the latter is ongoing. As for experiences of endangerment, they were constant throughout my youth. On this, likely my final day or thereabouts as an elderly man, let me regale you with a brief recounting of my early years. I was born over a month prematurely on Christmas Eve 1870, my mother dying right there and then before she even had time to hold me in her arms – my father, a cruel man used more to thrashing than hugging, would delight in informing me thusly. That he died an agonising and humiliating death from a genitalia-rotting disease he'd caught from Mimi the travelling prostitute when I was but eight, was truly a blessing. My lasting memory of my father is a horrid smell and an annoying noise as he shat and spat into a bucket beside his deathbed. Now, here I was an orphan and ready to work full time in my uncle's tweed factory. He was a widower, and didn't really need or want another child in the house.

The hours were long, the pay was nonexistent and I quickly developed a hunched back and crippled fingers. Uncle Joe would regularly order me to take my clothes off before proceeding to beat me with his belt after work, saying it was payment for my lodgings and food. The food, when I got any, were the leftovers off the rest of the family's plates. Usually my cousins would ensure they finished their dinners so that I didn't eat. Still, the brown water and whatever I could pinch from the animals' troughs usually sufficed. Cousin Agatha, Uncle Joe's only daughter, would sometimes make an exception and leave me her stale crust. I would eat it in excitement, knowing that her beautiful thick pink lips had been near it. In spite of this lack of nourishment I grew into a strong young man, due mainly to all the hard work I put in at the factory. And, sheer luck. Though my back remained arched and my fingers severely warped, I was particularly tall and most people didn't seem to notice any deformities.

Uncle Joe lost his three sons before they turned fourteen; two to bouts of a mystery sickness. The third, feeling left out, promptly threw himself in front of a cart one afternoon whilst at market. The wheels made a terrible mess of his smooth face, and the authorities advised Uncle Joe not to come himself but to send me to identify the body so as to remember his darling son as he was. The body looked terribly sad, but I told Uncle Joe that he had looked peaceful. Left with only a daughter, Uncle Joe drew up a new will and made me the main beneficiary. I was to get everything, he told me, and to earn this I had to marry Agatha when she turned sixteen. I was already sixteen, she was just fifteen. She did not seem best pleased at the arrangement, but I didn't complain. We could make it work, even though we were cousins and had really grown up as brother and sister. Things instantly eased up for me and I was allowed to join the family in the main house, away from my room in the barn.

Two weeks later, we three were sitting having breakfast when Uncle Joe came over all queer. All the colour drained from his face and he looked up to the heavens. Giving out a big groan, his face slammed onto the table and into his food. I leapt up, pulling him up to see what the matter was. And, as the porridge slipped from his cheeks and down his neck, I knew it was no good; he was dead. Agatha wept stoically, maintaining her reserved gait. The early morning sun caught her perfect face and I couldn't help but stare. Displeased at my attention, especially as I was clutching her father's dead body, she scorned me for my sins with a cuttingly cold stare.

I was now the owner of the factory, and my speedy rise bred disquiet amongst my workers. I had once been amongst them, but now that I was telling them what to do they were not too happy. Resentment was quick to surface and I found it difficult to establish my authority. One such worker, Jack Ffoulkes, had toiled alongside me all my years at the factory. He was a year older and had to some extent taken me under his wing. I would not say we were friends, for I knew not what friendship entailed, but we oft had shared private conversations to make the time in the factory more bearable. He had long heard me speak of the cruelty of my deceased father, and my appreciation for cousin Agatha's physical beauty and quiet aloofness. One day he had come to my uncle's house and seen Agatha for himself. I saw the way he looked at her, and she at him, and I never again spoke of her to him. Now that my uncle was dead, and I was the only thing in Agatha's way, Ffoulkes took it upon himself to let me know how he truly felt about her.

He came into my office one morning with a fierce look on his face, and I didn't take my eyes off him. I knew not to, for had I it would have shown weakness to him. He stood very quiet and very still, his chest going in and out, in and out.

'What do you want, Ffoulkes?' I asked him.

'The workers aren't happy, Aubrey,' he snorted back.

'I was *never* happy as a worker. What is your point?'

'Are you happy now?' he grunted, stepping closer. I too moved closer to him, our faces almost touching. He was tall like me, and we met on equal physical terms. 'Happy that you have Agatha all to yourself?'

'Wouldn't you be?' I put to him. His face reddened and I prepared for his fist to meet my person. However, my defiance appeared to unsettle his bullying stance and he backed off, storming out of the room. I relaxed, sitting down. Suddenly he appeared again at the door.

'I want her,' he said smugly. 'And, I'm going to get her.' He disappeared, leaving me alone once more. I stayed seated for a moment, wondering why my entire life had been a struggle. I wasn't particularly harmed by it in any serious manner, but it was a trifle trite to have to keep dealing with these challenges. I got to my feet and approached the window, looking down into the courtyard below. Ffoulkes came out of the building and jogged out of the gates. I just knew he was on his way to Agatha. Quickly I wondered what to do to make her mine and not his, for I had lost everything else in life. Yes, I had her father's factory which brought financial security; but I wanted the love and affection of his daughter too. He had promised it to me, and I wasn't going to let somebody take it away. Ffoulkes was the one who stood in my way. I decided the only way to deal with him was to fight fire with fire, and I instinctively punched myself in the face. Blood wept from my nose as I repeated the action numerous times, before I made for the ground floor to leave the building and get to the lovely Agatha.

* * *

I arrived as he was banging on the door. He hadn't seen me, so I held back behind the hedge at the bottom of the path for a moment to hear what he had to say to her. She must have been reluctant to open the door, as he was commanded to thrash again at it. Eventually the door did open.

'I have come straight from the factory,' the romantic gushed, 'walked away from my work in order to tell you my true feelings.'

'Master Ffoulkes, what do you mean by this indecency?' she replied in haste.

'I love you, fair Agatha, and I want your hand in marriage so that we can express our passion together.'

Such drivel nearly emptied my stomach of the morning's meal. Though, having led almost my entire life so far on scraps of food, now that I was eating well my stomach was often unsettled.

I peeped around the hedge and saw him bent down on one knee, her hand in his. No more of this hiding, I thought, and showed myself. As I marched to the pair, Ffoulkes got up and turned to face me.

'Oh Darren, what has happened to you?' Agatha gasped, dropping her usual decorum and coming to me. She looked up at my bloodied face, placing her hand on my cheek.

'Is this the man you truly want to marry, Agatha?' I said, waving my hand over at him.

'What? No!' she cried out, 'never did he do this, surely?'

'You cannot seriously be accusing me of hitting you,' Ffoulkes laughed.

'I am sorry that you find humour in my pain,' was my reply.

'Go,' she shouted at him, 'leave us.'

'These are lies, Agatha, lies,' he shouted back, trying to get to her. I blocked his way, smirking at him when my face was shielded from her gaze. He turned and went as Agatha and I stepped into the house.

'And don't come to the factory anymore,' I called after him, 'there is no job for you there now.' I slammed the door shut, locking it.

* * *

Later on, after Agatha had cleaned me up, she settled down by the fire to do some sewing. She wasn't very good at it, having had no mother to teach her, but she got by. I watched her from the doorway for a while, thinking I could not be seen in the dim light. However, she must have sensed my presence as her shoulders stiffened and her hands were shaking.

'Do you love Ffoulkes?' I decided to ask her.

'Come and sit down,' she responded, her usual reserved, quiet voice returned.

I did as she had asked, coming to sit across from her by the fire. 'Do you love Ffoulkes?' I asked again, more pronounced, determined to get an answer.

'I do not know what love is,' was her whispered reply. Nor did I, so I couldn't very well have accused her of lying. I wanted to, but I thought it best to play for sympathy rather than fear and resentment. I had seen my competitor off, and was stronger for it.

We sat in silence for a time, she struggling to complete her sewing under the dim light. Eventually she slammed it down on her lap and sighed. 'Why must it be women who have to sew?' she huffed. I didn't reply, instead catching her eye as I pretended to be rather uncomfortable in the armchair. 'Are you-'

'I am fine,' I shot back, holding my chest. 'He struck me in the chest as well, is all. It is aching.'

'Here, let me look at it,' she said, setting her sewing down on the table beside her chair and kneeling before me.

'No, I am ashamed,' I went on.

'Ashamed of what?'

'That I let him beat me – I should have had a go back at him.'

'Nonsense,' she smiled, looking rather delightful against the grey-orange glow of the smouldering fire. 'I am not one to go after brutes. Now, let me take a look.'

I unbuttoned my shirt and opened it as she placed her warm hand on my chest. 'Are you in the habit of going after *me*?' I asked coyly, looking into the fire.

'You'll live,' was her only reply as she quickly moved back to her chair and renewed her effort with the sewing. 'It's late, time for bed soon.'

She was beyond perfection in my eyes, truly that which I desired most in life right now. If only she would have me willingly, we could make a happy life here. Uncle Joe had promised her to me, but it would make it all the more pleasant were she to accept it. Today I felt I had progressed in the right direction, and tonight we had been closer than ever before. The distance between us all the years gone by could work in my favour; she might perceive me less as a brother figure and more of a lover. There was no real rush, I certainly had time to mould her. But, as had been seen with Ffoulkes, she was an attractive potency for male suitors. There was nothing else for me to do other than warn them off and isolate her for my own desires. This I would do, and we would come together in matrimony.

She went to bed first, and I did wonder whether or not this was an invitation for me to join her. However, as I approached her bedroom door and peeped through the crack in it, I could see she had fallen asleep. I did not rush off, instead wishing to look upon her for a while longer whilst she did not know that I was. She looked so serene, so short of worries and sorrows. Not even the pillowcase looked worthy of holding the weight of her head.

* * *

That night, a dream seized me in slumber. It was my own birth, laid down in plain sight for me to witness as a bystander. It was as though I was peering through my father's eyes, as if I was my own father watching myself being born. Mother looked so young and so fragile, no sound coming from her as those around her called out for her to push. She was unresponsive, hardly there at all, as I emerged from within her. When I was fully out, my mother was gone and I was whisked away from her. Then, something altogether otherworldly appeared in place of me – a huge, black box stood upright as all of those persons present dropped to their knees around it.

I wakened with a start, sitting up in bed and pondering my situation. If only my mother had lived, things may have been different. Fate had, nonetheless, conspired to make me the wealthy owner of a factory and set with waiting bride before I had even left my teenage years. Still, you always want what you cannot have.

* * *

I was sitting in Uncle Joe's chair at the table eating my breakfast when Agatha walked in. She looked tired and withdrawn, her usual fresh colour drained somewhat.

'You're late getting up,' I said scornfully. 'Miss Coombs has finished preparing food and moved on to cleaning.'

'I can make my own breakfast.'

'Here,' I shot back, 'let me.' I stood up and presented the chair for her to sit down in.

'I'm not sitting in *that* chair,' she replied, shaking momentarily as though a shiver had shot down her spine. She pulled her usual chair out next to it and she sat down.

'I will make your breakfast,' I said, heading for the bread.

'I'm perfectly capable of making it myself. In fact, I don't know why we hire Miss Coombs. I am sitting about this place all day, twiddling my thumbs.'

'Your father left us well in pocket, we can afford such simple luxuries as a housemaid.' I sliced some bread and placed it on the table before her.

'I'm not hungry,' she said defiantly, pushing it away and flopping back in her chair.

'Troy,' I called out to the dog, and faithfully he came running over. He was but two years old, a scruffy big wire-haired bearded thing with devilish floppy ears. We had not found him – he had found us. As I fed him the bread and patted his thick black coat, I perhaps knew what friendship was after all. He, practically swallowing the makeshift meal whole, licked my fingers and wagged his tail. I turned back to Agatha and puzzled over what to say next. She was still here, not having stormed off to some other quarter of the house, so I assumed she wished to continue this discussion. So, I came to sit back down next to her. 'We could really make this work.' I placed my hand on hers, and she did not pull away. 'I love you.' Now she pulled away.

'I am not some object to be passed down from my father to you.' She stood up and turned her back to me, but still did not leave the room. I too stood up, placing my hand on her shoulder. Her silk blouse was as soft as her skin.

'You are not some object to me, you are Agatha.'

'Women are like second class beings in this world, no better than a dog to some.'

'For so long I myself lived like a dog,' I went, tears

forming in my eyes. 'I was kept outside by your family, your father beating me when he liked and your brothers ensuring I lived off the most horrid of foods.' I let go of her shoulder, turning away. I heard her move to face me. 'But you, Agatha, you were the only one who gave me your bread. Admittedly it was just the crust, but it was enough to make me fall madly in love with you.' I turned back to face her, she now standing so close. 'You see, we are just the same. We both suffer hardships in one way or another; we just have to pull through.'

She stayed close to me, looking up into my eyes. I took my chance, leaning in to kiss her. Quickly she fled, bolting from the room. I did not go after her, but I felt good about the situation. She was coming around to the idea of she and me, and there wasn't much more work to do to convince her. I sat back down, stroking Troy as he placed his head in my lap.

* * *

I was late to arrive at the factory that morning, and so it appeared were most of the workers. I threw my weight around on the factory floor, demanding to know what was going on from the few who were actually there. It appeared Ffoulkes had drummed up a bit of support against me, though they had not showed themselves to protest. I went to my office, quite happy to replace the missing workers with new ones. Work was scarce, workers were ten a penny; I would soon find more. And, if not, I could easily get some of the new machines in to do it instead. In fact, that would be more ideal profit-wise. Ffoulkes had done me a favour. Moments later, he himself walked into my office and closed the door behind himself.

'Ah, Ffoulkes. I wondered when you would show

yourself,' I said to him, remaining seated behind my desk. In a way I felt I had already known that he would show himself at that moment – that I had foreseen it. 'Lost a few pals their jobs, I see.'

'You made a mistake having Agatha think I hit you,' were his quiet, grunted words.

'On the contrary.' I grinned at him, knowing I had succeeded and he had failed.

He came charging at me, grabbing me by the scruff of the neck and tossing me onto the floor. I was taken by surprise, unable to fight back as he kicked me about the stomach and head. I fell into unconsciousness, awakened only by the searing heat of a blazing inferno around me. I coughed, keeping my body to the floor as my lungs filled with smoke. I felt strangely cold as the sweltering flames billowed around my office, crawling to the door and struggling to open it. I stumbled out into yet more smoke and flames. The fire was everywhere – the entire factory ablaze and I far from escape. How I managed it I do not know, but I just kept on going until I had reached safety outside. A lesser man may have succumbed to the flames, but it was able to emerge with my life intact. Panic was all around, workers and passers-by alike gawping at the carnage. I turned to face the factory, *my* factory, dropping to my knees as I looked on helplessly. I put my hands to my face and it felt all wet and sticky.

* * *

The fire had scarred my face. As I lay in bed, Agatha tended the healing wound across my left cheek. She peeled back the dressing and dabbed the scars with a damp rag.

'I must look hideous to you now,' I said, lying there beneath her in my stupor.

'I was never attracted to you,' she said coldly, continuing her nursing duties. I took her hand and held it tightly, looking her deep in the eyes.

'You really *can* do anything, I don't know what I'd do without you,' I cooed.

'You'd find another woman to do your bidding, is what you would do. We're just tools to you men.'

'No, not at all.'

Silence came back, she finishing her duties before leaving me alone. I lay there and thought about things. The factory could be rebuilt, yes, but my relationship with my fellow workers could not. Still, they were no longer my fellow workers; I had climbed up, above them, and they were not pleased. Ffoulkes had obviously made an impression on them, and it made clear that he was not the only one displeased by my moving away from their ilk. Perhaps there was the sense that I had not earned my place as their superior, or that they did not think me fit. I had certainly shown my fitness for work alongside them for the last near ten years. Could they not be happy for me? Could they not be happy that one of their own had succeeded in life? The answer was no, they were not happy for me. I had not even been given a chance.

It was not as though I had strolled into my position as boss over them. My life had not been an easy stroll, in fact it had been quite the opposite. I lay here now feeling somewhat of a self-made man. It was me, and only me, who had sneaked into the house as a young boy and taken books out to the barn from Uncle Joe's collection. There, I had taught myself how to read; and I read well. I devoured all of his, albeit limited, library and felt at a distance from my fellow workers at the factory. That I was related to the boss already set me apart, giving me an unwanted air of distrust in their eyes. In a sense I did feel part of them, but also apart. I wanted to belong; I had never belonged anywhere or to anyone before. None of the other boys could read, and I did try to teach one or two of them, but it was not to be. They were not for moving forward, learning that which lay just beyond their current position. If they wanted to wallow in the gutter, let them; but I was not about to lie down and go willingly with them. No, I was going to fight them all and bring them to their knees. I was above them, greater than them. Ffoulkes was already a fallen man, now on the run from justice like the rat he was.

I tried to get up from the bed, but I was still too sore. Agatha's words had hurt me somewhat. To know outright that she had never been physically drawn to me, however, was not as bad as it sounded. That I would likely be left scarred by Ffoulkes' antics, then, didn't matter as much as it might have done. Sometimes I thought Agatha never found any man appealing, not even Ffoulkes. Oh, he was handsome, yes; well he *was*, but his murderous actions had shown him in his true ugly light. I, in my goodness, could grow on Agatha. But, as I said, I didn't think the physical was that much of a concern to her. What she truly wanted was *real* love and passion – love and passion that went beyond mere flesh and bone. I had read about such women in Uncle Joe's books. Oh yes, he thought those books had been written by men but I knew differently. It was clear women had been the true authors, with such strong self-assured women as central. Agatha was such as they: headstrong, defiant, uncompromising. It would be the ultimate challenge – the ultimate performance – for me to get beneath that and let her see in me what she wanted from a lover. And, I had ample time in which to do it; I had arranged with Miss Coombs to fetch what we needed from market. Agatha was to stay here and attend to me throughout my recovery.

The door pushed open at this moment and I eagerly looked up for Agatha. It was not she, but Troy the dog. He was looking for some food and I had but a morsel of bread left to give him. He sat obediently by my bed waiting for me to hand it to him. When I did he was overcome with thanks, licking me and pawing as payment. I stroked his beard and his long hairy black tail swished at the mat on the floor. There was such unconditional acceptance of who I was from Troy, that he reminded me of how I had seen both my father and Uncle Joe. They had beaten me, yes, but I had taken it and accepted it for what it was. I was not mentally scarred by it, I felt only a disappointment in their lack of verbal skills over violence. They had known no difference, clearly, and that was that. I knew a difference, and would not take the same course of action myself when Agatha and I were to bring children into this world. As I moved sideways and let Troy jump up to lay beside me on the bed, I felt rather sleepy. He put his head on my chest and I rested my hand on his paw, and we fell asleep together.

* * *

I was wakened by piercing shrieks and screams and didn't know where I was. Was it morning or night? I could not tell, but struggled to my feet and lunged towards the door to investigate. Troy had already gone and was now barking. I got into the hallway outside my room and Miss Coombs came crashing into me in hysterics.

'Oh Lord,' she wept, clasping her hands together, 'be with us now if thou truly exist!'

'What is it, woman?' I yelled back, pondering upon slapping her about the face to get some order.

'Agatha, oh Agatha!' she sobbed, collapsing onto the floor. I pushed her aside with my leg and struggled to

Agatha's room, throwing the door open. There she was, naked and hanging from one of the beams. Oh what horror! With renewed strength from perhaps The Lord himself, I galloped over and grabbed hold of her, pushing her upwards to ease the weight of her body on the rope around her neck. She felt so cold, yet soft, and I thought even in this position how sublime she looked. This was my first proper sight of her naked, and I was not at all displeased.

'Miss Coombs,' I yelled, 'Miss Coombs!'

She appeared at the door, unable to look upon Agatha and me. 'Master, she be dead, taken by her own hand.'

'She's still breathing,' I called back, seeing each struggling gasp escaping from between her lips. They had lost all of their pink – a horrid bluish tinge coming to them. 'Go fetch a knife to cut her down, for God's sake!'

Miss Coombs did so, and before long we had her down on the bed. She would not respond, lost in some other world. I looked down at her body once more, before covering it over with two thick blankets.

'I must go to the village for the doctor,' Miss Coombs cried, about to leave the room.

'No,' I said firmly, grabbing her arm and pulling her back.

'Master, she be very sick and you are far from recovered yourself.'

'I said no,' I insisted, 'they'll take her away. She will be prosecuted.'

'She may die if a doctor does not come.'

'I will treat her,' I said confidently.

'You?' she came back at me, almost laughing through her tears. 'You couldn't even save your uncle's factory, let alone fair Agatha here.'

'What did you say? Am I supposed to be able to fight flames with my bare hands?' I growled at her.

'I'm sorry Master, but you are still just a boy, and it is not for you to say what is best for Agatha.'

'I am old enough to know what I want and how to get it,' I shouted at her, turning back to check Agatha's breathing. It was weak, but still there. 'Besides, it is certainly not *your* place.' She darted out of the room. 'Miss Coombs!' I yelled. I struggled after her, catching her at the top of the stairs and pulling her back. Struggling to get away, she turned and slapped me across the face. In my desperate rage to save Agatha I lashed out in defence, sending poor Miss Coombs tumbling down the stairs. It was over in a second when she came crashing to the bottom with a big slam on her head. But, I didn't have time to attend to *her*, I had to get back to my Agatha.

* * *

It wasn't a good idea to push Miss Coombs down the stairs. It wasn't an idea at all. It had just happened, and there was no undoing it. I checked and she wasn't dead, but she wasn't far from it. I had a problem though, and this was that she wanted to go and fetch somebody to attend to Agatha. If she did that, Agatha would be prosecuted for the suicide attempt. I might in some way be incriminated also. I was certainly incriminated in the half-death of Miss Coombs at the bottom of the stairs here, so her still being alive right now was cause for mild alarm. She was lying on her back, facing up at me with her eyes closed. Unlike Agatha, who was young and full of potential ahead, Miss Coombs had had her day. She was into her fifth decade of existence now, and had never married. Her life was just what she led here with us, which was rather sad, and nobody would miss her.

Troy watched as I filled a bucket with water and

brought it into the hall beside Miss Coombs. I rolled her over onto her stomach and lifted her body over the bucket, dropping her head in it. There I left her to drown, going back up the stairs to check on dear Agatha. Damn Miss Coombs and her antics, I thought! Upstairs, Agatha lay rather still, the bruising on her neck looking very sore. I too felt very sore, wishing my sleep had not been disturbed by Miss Coombs' irritating howls. But, in a way I was glad she did waken me as Agatha may well have been up there too long and died. She looked rather serene on the bed, the pink returning to her lips. I leant over the bed and kissed her on them, and she did not flinch. In fact, I could almost see them creasing into a smile. It could not be, surely? Perhaps she was glad I had just kissed her and wanted me to do it again. I did so, staying upon them for longer this time. She did not move, but I could feel her breath entering my lungs. It felt like a new lease of life for me, as though it was she saving me from the brink of death and not the other way around. And also, I wanted to again look at her naked body. It was just under the blankets, just waiting there to be looked at. I held back, though, stepping away from her and thinking quite rightly that it would not be the correct thing to do. Clearly she was not well and had been driven to take such drastic action. Why indeed had she wished to commit suicide, and why naked? I didn't dwell on this for too long, instead being reminded of my main problem at this very moment as I stepped back into the hallway up the stairs. I looked down them, spotting Miss Coombs at the bottom – her head still in the bucket of water. A part of me wanted her to have vanished from my life and not be causing me this added problem, but it was not going to happen. A concerted effort was now required to dispose of the woman, and it would not be easy – she was not a tiny thing.

At this moment I thought that, were I to have to leave

the house to deal with Miss Coombs, I would be leaving Agatha alone. She may well come about during my absence and again attempt to inflict harm upon herself. I didn't want this – I didn't want this at all. I went back into her bedroom and, using the same rope she'd used to hang herself, tied her hands together and to the headboard of the bed. That way, she would be safe. She could not do harm to herself and, in doing so, do harm to me. She, above all others, was the person I least wished to lose in my life.

* * *

Miss Coombs' fat corpse was in the wheelbarrow. How I had managed to get her in it I do not know, but I had and in a way I was proud of my achievement. I remembered, one Christmas as a small boy when my father was still amongst us, sitting on her knee during a family visit to Uncle Joe's. That each Christmas was marred by my father's constant reminders of it being this time of year I killed my mother during birth, was but a small price to pay for being able to secure some small female contact. In fact, Miss Coombs was the first woman who touched me and let me touch her. Father always told me to stay in the outhouse when his lady callers came around, and so I was never to experience any physicality with them. Miss Coombs was, then, perhaps the closest I ever got to having a mother. She was no mother to me, of course, but in her own small way she had indirectly acted in that role in some minute way. There I sat, as a young boy upon her knee, for all the world thinking I had struck gold for but a fleeting moment. Little did I know that, a few years later, I would be puzzling over whether or not to cut those same legs off in an attempt to dispose of her body. These things do happen, however, and certainly to me.

I came to the edge of the bank and looked around. There was no sight of anybody but myself and Miss Coombs' corpse for miles around. In an instant I tipped the wheelbarrow forward and sent her on her way down into the river. She rolled quickly down the bank and hit the river with a splash, carried away by its speeding current. I had decided against cutting her up; partly through lack of energy, and partly through applied method. Were she to be found, her death could easily be explained as an accident. She could simply have come out here for a stroll and slipped. I would just report that she was missing, and wash my hands of the sorry affair. It was perfectly unavoidable, had she not acted in such a hysterical manner. Still, the past could not be unwritten and things were fixed as they were.

Troy looked down into the river, a little panicked, and started to struggle down the bank himself as Miss Coombs floated away. I called him back and he obeyed, returning with me to the house. I locked him in the study downstairs and went to check on Agatha. She must have come to life when I was out and struggled to get free as her wrists were very red and sore. Luckily she had not succeeded, and was now sleeping. She looked so happy to me, no stress registering on her features at all. One of her breasts was showing from beneath the blankets and her feet were protruding from the bottom. I stood there in silence and just watched her, so sorry for what had happened of late. None of it was in any way my fault, of course, but I was going to have to deal with all the problems. I just felt so distant from everything right now, as though I wasn't really connected to the here and now. I had often felt this way, and decided it was not the done thing. To push these ideas to the back of my mind was the more ideal action, especially in these circumstances.

Agatha's exposed breast was a sight to behold. I wished to hold it, seize it in a passionate embrace as our bodies became one. It reminded me how I had never had the benefit of my mother's milk as a baby, and this made me even keener not to see Agatha suffer death. She would not leave me, she *could* not; with her hands bound to the bed up here she was mine and only mine, and nobody else but the dog would be here at the house now. Yes, poor Miss Coombs I thought, but that was in the past now. All things had to come to their end eventually, but Agatha and I had yet to begin.

* * *

That night, as I plotted my statement regarding Miss Coombs' disappearance, I had the urge to sample some of Uncle Joe's wine. I stumbled down into his cellar deep beneath the house with only a candle as my companion and found what I had hoped lay down here. A vast row of untouched bottles, inches deep in dust, lay in wait for my consumption. This was the first time I had ever been down here, but I knew my uncle had enjoyed his wine. Now it was *my* wine, just like his daughter was mine, and I picked up a bottle and dusted it down. It was thirty years old already, and I opened it there and then. Sitting down on a crate, I swigged straight from the bottle and before I knew it the contents were gone from it. Another bottle was sought out, and I repeated the process. It made me rather merry to begin with, as I thought upon all the good in the world. I thought about Troy and all the pleasure he had given me from a mere pup in the barn to this very evening as he did everything I told him to. As I continued to drink, however,

I was reminded of the bad that had occurred over the years. Miss Coombs was gone from my mind during this remembrance, instead it was filled with all the beatings I had received first from my father and then from Uncle Joe. I smashed the empty wine bottle in anger, taking a large gulp from the nearly empty one in my hand. Something just wasn't right about it, when I gave it a bit of thought, and I somehow felt I'd been wronged. This was perhaps the first real time I had reached these heightened emotions regarding the treatment I had received and I truly began to feel hatred towards the two men. I was nothing like them, I was better than them. Even Ffoulkes, my own non-blood brother from the factory, had turned on me and dealt out his own physical abuse. However, I was the one who was still here on God's fair Earth and in control of my own destiny. I would rise up, literally, from the ashes of the old factory and rebuild it with renewed authority. I would show no weakness, no hint of compassion to those who tried to wrong me. Ffoulkes had taken me by surprise, but nobody else would be afforded the same leniency. For too long I had been my father's son; weak-willed, complacent and nondescript. I was nothing like *he*. I was my own man, and would succeed where he had failed. Granted, his biggest failing was in dying, and I had almost been as foolish to allow this to happen to me during Ffoulkes' assault in the factory. Nothing, and nobody, would be given a similar chance. Miss Coombs could have proven to be my downfall, but I had disposed of her; and Agatha, who lay upstairs in the house above, could potentially attempt unwarranted tomfoolery again. If only there was some way to save her from herself, and keep her with me as my own. She would come around to the life I'd provide for her eventually – it was just a matter of waiting patiently for that to happen. I looked around the cellar, swishing my candle from side to side to get a better look at the space around me. It was then, as my drunken head loped lazily from side to side, that I struck upon the perfect method in which to enact my wish – Agatha would come and live down here in the cellar. Away from harm's way in the world beyond this closed environment, we could build the perfect life together. Fate had granted me continued existence in spite of life's tough tribulations, and I was not going to throw it away in idiocy. At that very moment a very brief vision of something else flashed through my mind – something away from this time and place. I myself, and not Agatha, was hanging in a long line with many other men. Next I was alive again and manically stabbing at a man and slitting his throat. I was perplexed, incensed, at these apparitions attacking me.

* * *

Agatha screamed in terror and begged me to stop as I dragged her, hands and feet bound, down into the cellar. It was quite the struggle as she fought my weakened body, managing to bite my arm as we came to the bottom of the cellar steps. My head was pounding and my mind was not clear, so I lashed out at her and caught her across the face with my fist. This sent her to the floor and stopped her screams. Now she just moaned as I fumbled my way back up the steps to fetch the candle. When I came back down I could see her just lying there, her head resting on the broken wine bottle. Quickly I went to her, putting the candle aside and pulling her head up. I rested it on my knee and pressed my finger to her lips.

'I am so sorry,' I cried, real tears coming from my eyes. I was so upset to think I had struck my poor girl. 'What must you think of me?' She did not reply as I stroked her hair and studied the cuts the broken bottle had made to her cheek. 'Now we are the same,' I remarked, a burning sensation pulsing from my own scarred face. 'I will heal you, just like you healed me.'

Again I went up the steps into the house, filling the bucket I'd drowned Miss Coombs in with water and taking it down to Agatha with a cloth. Gently I cleaned the blood from her cheek.

'Why are you doing this?' she suddenly asked me, sounding quite forlorn.

'It is for your own good, Agatha. You cannot be allowed to die by your own hand.'

'There is nothing left for me here, my life is unbearable.'

'No more will it be so,' I spoke with increasing happiness as I took hold of her head with both my hands. 'I love you Agatha, and we will lead the most wonderful life together.'

'I don't want that,' she spat back, appearing to me, only briefly, as rather ugly. It must have been how the candlelight flickered in the slight breeze coming down the steps, and because of this I wanted to seal her in to stop what it was making me see. Her face remained creased and contorted in such an unsatisfactory countenance that I moved away from her briefly. 'You are drunk, you have no right to bind me like this,' she continued with her misplaced venom.

'You have no choice.'

'Where is Miss Coombs?' she demanded.

'Gone to get ointment for your sore neck.'

Now I moved back to her, running my finger along the mark left by the rope on her neck. I was perhaps a little nervous, my hand shaking as I gently touched her flesh. She looked up at me leaning over her, taking in her naked body with my heavy eyes. They felt weighted, yes, as though some fiend had stuck hooks in them and were trying with all their might to hoist them from their sockets. I rubbed hard at them as Agatha coughed.

'You are not well, Darren,' she strained through her coughing. 'You have come over all queer.'

'You have driven me thus,' said I to her silly talk. 'Had you not got caught up in that noose then we would not be where we are now.'

'Had you left me there, we would not be where we are now,' was her adamant rebuttal as she gritted her teeth at me.

She had looked so beautiful up there, hanging from the noose in Nature's unsheathed outfit, that leaving her there could have delivered a level of visceral pleasure to me. But, I wanted her alive so badly that she just had to come down. Down she most certainly *had* come, further down at this very moment than she ever had been before in her entire life. The cellar was not the most comfortable of places, but it was still a part of the house and this was the house we were to make our life together in. There was no escaping that now.

'I would not wish any harm to come to you,' I whispered softly to her, leaning closer in to her soft and bountiful lips. 'I am sorry that I struck you, but you were acting out of turn.' I touched her cut cheek and she winced. 'I love you, Agatha.' My hand instinctively came to rest on her breast, the same one I had looked at earlier whilst she slept. It was my first proper touch of it, and I did not move my hand from its initial resting place at first. It felt rougher than it looked, and less firm than I had expected. I kissed her and felt her try to pull back, but there was no space to pull back into. She was now shivering. 'Are you cold?' I asked her, undoing the buttons on my shirt with my spare hand as the other remained on her breast. When my shirt was fully open, I took my hand away from her to remove it, thinking at first to lay it down upon her body. But, had I done that her body would then be hidden from view. I did not want that at all and, as I looked down at her looking up at my exposed chest, I felt she did not want that either.

* * *

It had been near nine months now, and Agatha was heavily pregnant. I was doing my best to keep her comfortable down in the cellar, and in some ways it was quite homely down there. The damp smell had not ceased, and I couldn't stay down there myself for too long at a time. Agatha had always had somewhat of a sickly chest, and I suppose the conditions in the cellar did not help this. But, there she had to remain; it had gone on too long now to just undo and go back to the way things had been. I still kept her hands bound, replacing the irritating rope with chain. She no longer complained about her hands, she just sort of lay there in a daze on the bed I had brought down for us. She no longer pulled away when I came to her either, because she knew she could not get away. It was no use resisting me, and in a way I felt we were making progress. We had certainly grown closer, and I knew this was in some part due to the fact I was the only person she saw now. She relied on me for everything, and did her best not to upset me anymore. I had been rather difficult, shall we say, during the first few weeks of her being down there, but I had mellowed with time and she had accepted her situation. However, the added factor of pregnancy had created an altogether greater level of challenge to our prolonged affair.

When we first realised she was pregnant, Agatha's first reaction was an uncontrollable hysteria. This was quickly replaced with an overriding desire that we be wed in the local chapel. I agreed at first, but I could never let go of that fear she would either try to harm herself again or worse – accuse me of some ill treatment towards her. I could not cope with such lies, especially as I above all others knew what actual ill treatment entailed. What I had done for Agatha was love and affection, not some kind of cruel torture. Gradually, as the months unfolded, I believe she began to agree with me. She certainly gave up on the idea of leaving here. Now, here I was ready to deliver our baby into the world and become a father myself. I would not repeat the mistakes of the past. I had had time to think about all the things that had happened to me in the past whilst I was recovering from the fire, and I could see that a lot of mistakes had been made by those around me. Luckily I was educated enough to realise I could break the cycle of abuse by acting differently. My child was soon to be born into the world, and I would be the perfect father. Agatha, too, could possibly rise up from her stupor once she saw me with our child and come to accept everything. As soon as I could be sure of her true acceptance, she would join child and me upstairs in the house again.

Miss Coombs was never mentioned now, and her body had never been found. At first, I had a few visits from various folks in the village expressing their concern regarding her departure; some even wished to speak to Agatha. Eventually they stopped asking, and seemed to see in me a rather pitiful figure whose luck had not been good. I rather enjoyed their pity, for it aided in my masking of the truth. I had never been a liar, but I could not afford to hang for Miss Coombs' benefit. Agatha needed me – she truly needed me – and now that child was soon upon us I was needed twice over. I thought about Miss Coombs often, of course, and how unfortunate her accidental demise had been. However, had she remained in the house I certainly wouldn't have been able to do as I had done with Agatha. I had free reign to do as I wished, and it was rather fulfilling.

As the hours got closer to the birth, Agatha got steadily more confused and withdrawn. When I did sleep, all that played in my mind was that dream where I had witnessed my own birth, and the ultimate death of my mother. The big upright box was in prominence, looming as a shadow over my life. Now I stood at the foot of a real bed, my love lying bound on it with her legs spread apart. I could see the child's head and froze still, the sudden realisation of what I had done to Agatha filling my conscience. She must have thought me monstrous to attempt suicide in the first place, and all I had done was continue to fuel that ill feeling by keeping her captive down here and trying to build a relationship. There was no going back now, and I rallied myself out of that wasteful mindset in order to deliver my child.

'Push,' I called out to her as I bent down to support the head. Agatha was not responding. 'Our child is coming, Agatha, you must make an effort.' She turned her head and looked up at me. I looked down at her and smiled. Her lips moved, but I heard no words. 'Push!' I called again. Her lips moved some more, but still no words could be heard. I leant over and pressed my ear towards them. No more did they move, but she gave an almighty push and I swept in to secure the newborn in my arms. There was one final gasp from Agatha before she fell silent, and I looked at her still face. I knew she had died, and it was all Miss Coombs' fault. Damn her!

I untied Agatha's dead hands and placed our son in them.

* * *

The next few days were wrought with difficulties as I dealt with my son alone. I felt Adam was a good name, and that was that. There was nobody to disagree with me or suggest other potential names. Towards the end of that first week there came a terrible smell from the door leading into the cellar. I hadn't been down there since coming up with Adam in my arms that first time after his birth, and Agatha would not be looking herself at all by now. I remembered how her brother, who'd tossed himself under the cart, had looked just hours afterwards and, although Agatha had not been mangled facially, the smell was a clear indication of the unfortunate processes now going on. Still, the smell became that much more intense within mere hours and there needed to be something done to stop it. I placed Adam safely in the cot I had made him with my own hands upstairs whilst his mother carried him in the cellar, and gingerly opened the door to go down there.

I did not dare to think what would meet my eyes as I progressed slowly down each step, clutching nervously onto a flickering candle. There was some small part of me that wanted to see an empty bed, an indication that Agatha hadn't in fact died but had manufactured a false demise in order to escape my clutches. But, no, there her rotting remains lay; her legs still spread apart and her arms positioned as though cradling a newborn. My vile actions came crashing down on me, a self-opinion growing that I was clearly deranged on so many levels. But, things *had* truly just escalated with one event after another. Was I to blame Miss Coombs, Ffoulkes, Uncle Joe, my father? Perhaps it was time to take the blame myself. After all, I had allowed things to unfold in this increasingly ill manner. Nevertheless, the end product of my actions was the baby

Adam, and I was certainly not going to allow him to turn into somebody as damaged as me. I would be the perfect father and do right by the boy. Once and for all, the cycle would be broken and he would grow up into a fine man. He and I had everything we needed to make this happen: a house, the newly rebuilt factory. Admittedly, there was no mother, but I was long overdue a new housemaid.

* * *

'Please, call me Emily,' was the first thing the petite young thing had said to me upon responding to my call for a housemaid. She was so, so wondrously perfect that I quite forgot about Agatha within a matter of seconds and set my sights on her. To say I fell head over heels in love would be a crass understatement, for my deep feelings for her knew no limits. After a fortnight in the house I had asked her hand in marriage and she had, surprisingly, accepted. She was the daughter of a poor woman, and her father was dead. Her mother came to live with us, and all three of us reared dear Adam together. We were quickly married and in a flash added siblings for my firstborn. All had come good in my life in the end, and I had done well in spite of my early challenges.

Emily's mother did eventually prove rather difficult as she advanced in years, as was to be expected. I remembered the speed and ease with which Miss Coombs had been dispatched, and did contemplate a similar fate for her. Luckily, Nature proved to be her assassin and I was spared the onerous indecency of putting her out of her misery myself.

The one true devastation in my life was the loss of Troy. Though Emily followed suit and succeeded him in his loyalty, I was so attached after his decade of service that when the time came to say goodbye I was overcome with grief. He, with his contemplative stoicism as he sat looking out onto the vast countryside beyond the house, was the greatest mind I ever came across. He knew it all, and had life well laid out under his paws.

I thought of Agatha often, and how sadly it had ended for her; but I overcame those feelings of guilt. No longer did I blame myself, and Emily just did as I wished. She was not for challenging my whim, she just wanted to please me. This, even as the years passed, never did thin one bit. There was just one occasion when she tried to probe the origins of Adam, and I had warned her away from prying. She never did query again. She enabled me to continue unmolested by both the law and my conscience for the rest of my days.

And so, here I am at the end of my days reminiscing on a brief, and unfortunate, portion of my early life. Adam would have grown into a fine young man, though sadly he had inherited some of his mother's headstrong urge for independence and, of course, her sickly body. He had a fit one day and died at fourteen whilst trying to "find himself" out in the fields. Still, all eight of the children Emily and I had together survive to this day. Emily herself also lives, though she spends much of her time sitting very still and very quiet in the corner of the room. She will spend hours upon end just staring into space, occasionally mumbling about "profound difficulties" and the like.

After my brief flash of upset and mischief at the beginning of my life, I have been able to create an entirely new existence free from trouble. I have lived a good life, and reached a vast age. In the end there was no stopping me, for no matter what challenges occurred I was able to overcome them unscathed. I know I only have days, if not hours, left to live, but it does not trouble me. Death is the surest of all life experiences, and the illness that has taken me down is not the most fiendish. The result is the same no matter what gets you, and acceptance of your mortality is crucial. The one thing on my mind as I prepare for the end is if I ever truly felt love for anybody. Looking over at Emily, I think of what Agatha's opinion of her would have been. All Emily has wanted to do in life is be a wife to a man. Agatha would have seen her as a weak sort of woman, a non-entity with no mind of her own. With that laid out, there is a part of me that feels less connected to Emily because of this. I don't know why I was drawn to Agatha, other than her physical beauty. The same attributes also drew me to Emily. My brute force was able to crush Agatha's desire to stretch out beyond the confines of what was expected of her sex. That was her downfall. My downfall, as a man conditioned throughout life to command with strength and deviousness, is mere old age.

As I draw my final breaths, I have the arrogant impression that they are nowhere near my final ones at all. There is the overriding urge to say I can see the large upright box just up ahead of me. Emily has certainly made no fuss of it – not that she has made much of a fuss about anything of late – and I myself am inclined to put it to the back of my mind. Its sudden presence now makes no sense, even though I find myself not questioning the coming of the box. It seems right.

I remember Troy's last day on Earth all those years ago when I was still a young man as though it was yesterday. I had to carry him out for his daily study of Nature by then, and gently placed him down in his favourite spot atop an old barrel. That day, he did not want to look far out into the distance – perhaps he no longer *could* see that far. No, his attention was seized by something close by and on the ground. I, curious, trained my own sight and spotted a large dandelion weed growing rather healthily in the path. I had dug it out so many times before, but it just kept coming back. I went then and tried to pull it, but it would not come. The roots were strong, and the leaves a vibrant green. It would go on growing in spite of the war against it.

A Confession, by Jack Ffoulkes

I've done a terrible thing, and it's changed my life for good; or, more accurately, for bad. You could say it has ruined my life, ensuring I will never ever have what I want. It concerns the most perfect of God's creations on this Earth: Agatha. Had I not acted so foolishly and spoilt what she and I had going, I would not be where I am right now. However, this whole thing did not just involve the two of us. One Darren Aubrey was the third in our triangle, her cousin and, by a twist of remarkable fate, my boss. He is younger than I am by several months, and, knowing exactly where he has come from, it is hard to accept him in this position after a sudden change. He did not help matters with his arrogant air. His greatest tool in bringing about my downfall was not work, though, but Agatha herself. He wanted her, and would not allow me to take her away.

I had, rather foolishly you might say, fallen desperately in love with her the moment I had fixed my sight upon her divine presence; Aubrey had been right in his assessment of her throughout our many long talks. We would speak casually on the factory floor when he worked alongside me, long before his uncle dropped dead, and Agatha was the main focus – that was until I showed an interest in her. His uncle Joe, or Mr Aubrey to me, had apparently promised his daughter's hand in marriage to "my friend", and this was the beginning of a very slippery slope into the cesspool of shame and regret I now wallow in. Yes, I had underestimated Aubrey's cunning in making Agatha believe I had hit him, but that was no excuse for beating him and burning the factory down. I have left him for dead mere hours ago, but had time to think upon my actions. This is my confession that I am as guilty as sin itself for the unspeakable loss of control that resulted in my killing of Darren Aubrey. He was a friend to me, and we part company due to the simplest of disagreements: a girl. Poor Agatha, I think of her now with the rest of her long life ahead of her, and am at least happy that two such cowards as Aubrey and me are no longer in it. I stand here, about to throw myself down into the river, and realise my love for Agatha is real. I love you, Agatha, but we can never be together.

JIM'S A PART OF APART

For me to have felt a part of something in life, I'd have had to have not been apart from things all my life. I always keep myself away, distanced. Goodness knows why. It's done me no good because here I am, carried off to war and thrust right into the action. Digging trenches sounds like a simple job. Let me tell you it is *not*. Nor is digging trenches an easy job. This is me being a part of something, something altogether bigger than anything else before it in the history of mankind. A war to end all wars they're calling it. It is hell on Earth.

They call me twitch – because I have a twitch. When I get excitable it gets worse, hence why it's going berserk right now. First my eye starts to spasm, followed by my cheek, then my entire face goes ballistic. It's a terrible nuisance, crippling even. I also cannot help but clear my throat all the time, even though it doesn't need clearing. I have to be careful however, as I end up clearing it or even coughing when those around me are doing the same. Mimicking the noises of those around me isn't going to do me any favours in the trenches. We're all so close, so very very close. Truth be told, this whole situation is downright dreadful. Sixteen of my 'fellow men' died in a truly terrible manner yesterday – a heavy downpour quickly filled their section of trench with water and they drowned. So did the rats. The rats are good company.

I am apart from things because I do not belong – neither

here in the trenches, nor to anywhere else. My part in the grand scheme of things is so minuscule and insignificant that I feel myself afforded nothing from anyone. My life story, if that is the correct phrase, just doesn't seem solid or interesting enough to relay to you. Young men like me are getting sent over the top of the trenches every single day and being instantly slaughtered. I will go soon, and I will not be sorry. There is absolutely no reasoning to it at all; not one that I understand anyway.

I feel so separate from life that I've begun to view things from outside my own body, looking down on myself as I go about my daily duties. I look foolish and clumsy, but that doesn't matter – there are many kinds a weakness on show if you know how to see it. There are cries for mother amidst the blizzard of bullets, and weeping over the simplest of issues that arise such as having to drink dirty water. I've also seen the strangest of strengths from the unlikeliest of people, but I simply cannot allow myself to accept it. If I do, I might have to try and emulate them. I'm not a very good performer. I've never been good at anything. Despite that, I have the very briefest moments of feeling great. Sometimes I just feel utterly great and superior to everyone else, but it is only a fleeting feeling that is soon replaced by my usual self-loathing.

It might sound like a cliché to say I don't belong here – in the trenches about to die for a cause I don't believe in – but I simply *do not* belong here. There is something else, something more to my life than this narrowness I am being presented with; my trouble is that I cannot put my finger on it. The only thing I *can* put my finger on is the trigger as I go over the top with my rifle. That is a certain. What if I freeze and cannot fire? No worries – even if I do fire I won't last long. It is a foolish endeavour.

Just that moment, as I am observing myself from above,

a huge vertical slit appears in front of me in the trench. As it opens, emanating a dull purple glow, a scentless breath wheezes out and a hand emerges. I cannot tell whether it is male or female, but it outstretches itself towards me. If I am to take it, will I be pulled through the slit? I step back, folding my arms, and the hand and slit vanish as quickly as they have arrived.

Before I know it I have a rifle in my hand and am being pushed up a wooden ladder. Bullets don't kill me – men kill me. Men like me, pulled from their lives and sent here to play soldier.

PETER'S TROUBLES

It came as a terrible shock to find myself presented with Him so soon. I was not a believer, but I played along – it was easier that way. If I was to impart one single piece of advice to another human being, it would be to always seek out the easiest option in life. Oh yes! There was nothing easy about coming face to face with the Führer himself.

I was born in 1925 – a good year apparently. Some old bag told me I'd picked an ideal period in history in which to exist. When I questioned her why, she just cackled and danced about on the spot. Stupid bitch. Nevertheless, I felt somewhat pleased with my slice of being for a time, having happily avoided too much trouble as a young boy. Of course, all that changed when I was 14 and the world went to war. We lived on a farm in Wales and quickly found ourselves housing some Italian prisoners of war. Nice chaps, really. Stole some china out of the cabinet, but owned up to it and accepted the lenient punishment. Anyway, things were alright for me for a while in terms of keeping out of the war – both in terms of my age and the fact I was working on the farm. I didn't do much work; I didn't need to. We had the Italians to do the heavy stuff.

Things altered dramatically one Monday morning in early 1945 when I awoke to the sight of a balding man standing over my bed. What remained of his hair was fair, darkened only by too much cream which plastered it to his bulging reddened head. The head only seemed so swollen on account of the rest of his body being so thin and lacking in presence. He placed a briefcase on the tallboy next to my bed in the small attic room and opened it, taking out a large syringe. Before I could come too properly, he had stuck it in my neck and I fell asleep once again.

* * *

Adolf Hitler – I was utterly terrified. He stood across from me in the low-ceiling room, staring into a full-length mirror. The only object that separated us was a large, pale chest lying flat on the floor. Several wires and a tube ran from it into an area to the left of me, curtained off and in darkness.

'I pulled many strings to bring you here,' he uttered in a low, almost not-there, voice. I felt like my voice would also be as weak; either due to nerves, or the damp air in here. I blinked, trying to adjust to the low lighting. 'Seven agents died to achieve my aim.' He watched his own lips as they moved. 'Their deaths are unfortunate. Good agents.' His English sounded at the very least understandable. I remained silent and deathly still, not quite sure even what position my body was in or whether or not I was bound. I felt utterly away from myself, or maybe I wished so. I watched in the mirror as Hitler reached into his jacket pocket with a trembling hand and brought out a tattered old notebook. It was yellow, falling to bits. His shaky, clawed hand lifted the thing to his lips and he kissed it as his hunched back quivered. 'Peter Smith.' He knew my name, he'd gone to great lengths to bring me here – why? I could not ask him. '*The* Peter Smith. You are the genuine article, your lineage has been traced.' He now turned to face me, struggling down on to one knee and bowing his head before me as he clutched onto the notebook. 'Save me, oh Great one,' he pleaded with me. Just then another man, in uniform and very tall, walked in unannounced. Hitler got up with some effort, screeched something in German to the man, and sent him running with his tail between his legs. 'Forgive me,' he uttered to me, the volume of his voice dropping once more. I stayed deadly still and quiet as he stepped closer, as if waiting for me to respond in some way. I knew not how to. His eyes briefly flicked over to the curtain before resting on the object on the floor between us. 'You have many powers. I know you see the future – you saw me as the murderer of millions of people. Your prophesy is somewhat accurate, though I am not their murderer. I sweep away the worthless filth. I am a cleanser.'

'You are an opportunist and an arsehole, Adolf,' I told him. I couldn't help myself, it just came flying out from between my lips. I awaited his onslaught.

'You are an affront to nature – to the very fabric of existence,' he calmly told me back.

He clicked his fingers and the curtain to the side of us retracted. A bright light came on and behind it stood a large black upright box – the wires from the pale horizontal box between Hitler and myself running into the back of it. Next to the box sat a very small bald man in white overalls. Behind him was some kind of control panel with buttons and levers, also connected by wires to the big upright box.

'What is all this?' I asked, gaining ever so slightly in confidence following Hitler's meek reaction to my last uttered phrase.

'Meet Alois Vadge,' Hitler told me, pointing at the little bald man on the stool, 'my chief medical advisor on this special day.' The word medical was certainly not what I wanted to hear from this man's lips. We'd all heard the news reports of what he and his Nazis had been up to. Here I now was, waiting to be used in another gruesome experiment. Alois Vadge stayed perfectly still and perfectly silent, save for a slight dilation of the nostrils as they kept the air flowing to his lungs. 'The third reich is crumbling – it is the story of my life,' Hitler went on. 'You work hard for something really nice, only for someone else to come along and spoil it.'

'Invading Russia didn't help you,' I pointed out.

'A tactical mishap, or divine intervention?' he mused, tapping his little moustache and swiping his greasy black side-parting back into place. 'Germany has failed me, I have ordered total destruction of Berlin. The only avenue left open to me is reincarnation and immortality – secrets you hold.' His trembling, clawed fingers waved in my general direction. He clicked those same fingers and Alois Vadge suddenly sprung up and dashed to the control panel behind him, fiddling with the knobs and levers. The pale box between Hitler and myself began to emanate a greenish glow. Condensation began dripping from it before Hitler leant over and wiped the top. It was misty, but there appeared to be some kind of body in there. Alois dashed across clutching a towel, which Hitler promptly snatched from him. After mopping his sweaty brow with it, and undoing a couple of catches on the side of the container, the two men pulled at the top, breaking a seal as the lid started to free. And then – the smell. A putrid odour raced out as the men pushed the lid aside and peered in. The big black box to the side just stood there, seeming to play no part other than playing host to wires and a tube. I too peered inside to see the image of a very tall and thin man sporting white curly hair. His cheeks were sunken, his eyes deeply set into his skull. His wrinkled hands lay across his chest. He was submerged in ice, which was melting around him. 'A familiar face, Peter Smith?'

I did not recognise this person, though some far off inclination told me that I should. 'Who is it?' I questioned, the horrors that Hitler had planned running through my mind.

'Nature would have asserted you never see this man again, yet he is before you now ready to be reanimated. He is Thaddeus Hobble, the man who secured your writings so that I could gain everlasting life. He has been dead two hundred years, his body kept frozen in deepest Siberia as per his wishes. My turn on Russia was not all to no avail.'

As the ice melted from his body, Hobble's hair became limp and fell from his scalp in clumps. His exposed head reacted with the muddy air and blistered, peeling off in patches. Hitler gently patted Hobble's face with the towel as Vadge reached in and lifted his arm up. He checked for a pulse, looking worriedly back at Hitler, before bending down and pulling the wires out from the container and placing the ends directly onto Hobble's temples. Sparks flew, some landing in the last of the water as it drained away underneath the inanimate man and causing mini explosions. I kept fixed, still unsure whether I could move or not. Hitler shouted something in German as he dropped to his knees and banged his fists on the floor. All at once the sparks stopped and Vadge leapt back as Hobble's eyes opened. His lips opened and a gasp of air released itself. Hitler pulled himself up against the container and leant in, his eyes moist and his mouth making some sort of grin. Hobble's body twitched and spasmed momentarily.

'He is alive,' he said to me.

'What now?' I wondered.

'We kill him,' Hitler responded bluntly. 'The process works, we have no further use for this man.' Suddenly Hobble's arm outstretched itself and slapped Hitler aside, knocking him to the floor. 'There is no muscle wastage – remarkable.'

The reanimated corpse sat himself upright and looked

sideways at me. His eyes widened before narrowing. 'I,' he uttered, his attempt at speech turning into a cough. Once his throat was cleared he hauled himself up and got out of his once-icy casket. He was naked, and Hitler studied the body intently. 'I saw you die,' he said to me, 'and yet you live.'

'You died as well, Hobble,' I responded without thinking, knowing somehow that some deep recess had provided these words. I looked behind the man to see that Hitler and Vadge were dancing together. Hobble turned to face them.

'Men of fancy,' Hobble laughed. They promptly stopped and both turned to face him. Hitler stepped up. 'Who are you, you ridiculous little man?' Hobble questioned, his attention drawn to his moustache. 'There is muck above your lip.'

Mirth had turned to fierce aggression on Hitler's face. 'I am the Führer himself, Adolf Hitler.'

'The imbecile from Peter Smith's fairy stories? What a turn of events,' Hobble responded glibly, becoming somewhat aroused. 'It appears my scheme to travel into the future has worked – what year is this?'

'1945,' I confirmed, trying to keep my eyes off his half-erection.

'The year of Adolf Hitler's suicide, the year he loses everything,' Hobble gloated.

'Incorrect,' Hitler yelled, raising a finger at the men. 'I may choose to fade from view for now, but I shall be back. If I cannot gain access to The Space through Peter's mind, then I shall merely have myself frozen in the same manner that was so successful for you.' Now Hitler smiled again. 'As for *you*, Thaddeus Hobble – the remover of your own wife's breasts – your purpose is complete.' He turned and nodded to Vadge, who brandished a concealed pistol from a strap on his waist. 'It has been proven the process of reanimation works, you can now be disposed of.'

With this, and a horrified gasp from Hobble, Vadge pulled the trigger and shot him in the face. Blood splattered over my own face and I went to wipe it off, now realising that my hands were indeed bound. I was completely weighted down, unable to move whatsoever. Hobble's unsheathed body dropped lifelessly to the floor as Vadge moved in and shot him another three times in the face at point blank range. After this, the pistol went back into its hiding place on Vadge's person and he strolled over to the console unit by the upright box. He flicked some switches, picking up and returning with some kind of helmet with wires running from it. He placed it on my head; it was small, so Vadge forced it down – pushing and pushing. I growled at him, but he did not cease. Then, when it was suitably fixed, he began turning some sort of bolts on it. Four razor-sharp pins in all, each drilling right into my skull. I cried out in sheer agony as thin blood ran from under the helmet and down my face and neck. I could feel my hair soaking wet under there, through blood and sweat, as Vadge stepped back to eye up his work. Suitably pleased with the balance of the device, he seemed to lose interest and instead went back to Hobble's body and dragged him away out of sight. My pain began to ease to a gentle numbness as my brain pulsed. Hitler, who had been standing still watching the whole time, again slipped his greasy side-parting back into place with crooked fingers welded onto a trembling hand.

Vadge reappeared with a syringe as Hitler leant in and undid my belt. Undoing my trouser button and unzipping my flies, the dictator pulled at my trousers as I just sat there in an incoherent mess. I looked down to see my trousers and underpants around my fastened legs as Vadge moved in with the big shiny needle.

'Advisor Vadge will now inject your scrotum with bull semen, Peter Smith,' Hitler explained calmly as my buttocks clenched and I pulled back as far as I could. It wasn't far enough, as I instantly felt the most agonising of stinging sensations. I opened my eyes for just enough time to see the last of the gloopy yellowy substance exit the syringe, and enter my own testicles. Finished, Vadge stepped away, and with a quick hand gesture was dismissed by his master. 'It will be processed along with your own semen.' Hitler slowly knelt down between my legs. 'I will draw out this elixir of potions – suck out and consume it so that I may benefit.'

I watched flabbergasted as he opened his mouth and stuck out his tongue, touching the tip of my flaccid penis with it. I couldn't feel it, I didn't want to feel it. Everything else that I'd heard this man was responsible for seemed distant to me, forgivable – it was this vile act against me that made him a monster now. My penis remained limp, lifeless, as he moved his head forward and it disappeared inside his mouth. Suck he did, with increasing ferocity as his right hand found its way inside his own trousers and he masturbated along. I became so overwhelmed that I gave way to the pure desire to cease existing and I shut myself down.

* * *

I woke up in a slump, the vague image of two Hitlers in front of me. One got down on his knees and began praying alongside a young woman with short brownish hair falling in curls atop and behind her head.

'Meet my wife Eva,' the standing Hitler called over to me as Vadge placed his pistol in the woman's mouth. 'We were married just yesterday.' He fired, her head popping as she dropped to the floor. Next, the gun turned to the other Hitler and he too was shot. Hitler again dismissed Vadge and I slipped back into incoherence.

* * *

The next time I woke up I was lying flat out in complete darkness. I went to get up but could not move more than an inch or two. Struggling to bring my arms from my sides to my head, I felt around directly above me. I was sealed shut inside some kind of hard wooden coffin, my lungs suddenly reminding me that I had no oxygen in here. I gasped for air, suffocating. It felt as though I had no mouth whatsoever as I used up the last of my energy to pound on my tomb. Nobody came to let me out – there was no sound at all from the outside. I must have been buried deep underground, I could feel the crushing weight of earth on top of my chest. I relinquished all desire to struggle and just lay there as still as a corpse, waiting to become one. My death was surely not that far off; I would at first fall into unconsciousness and then pass away. But, it did not come. I went on in utter desperation for air as I suffocated and suffocated in my little box. I was starving too, from the cold and from lack of food. My mouth, dry and flaking, just sagged open as my lungs worked tirelessly in search of any morsel of oxygen. Maybe I *was* dead, and this was what non-existence was. It was certainly hell, something I could endure no longer. But no, it went on and on. Unable to do anything but feel the pain of suffocation and starvation, I knew not of how little or how long had passed in time – all I knew was that it seemed like an infinite passage. On and on, endless concealment.

* * *

Oxygen has a flavour, a taste, and it filled my scabbed mouth as it tried to work further down into my lungs. I cannot describe the sensation, or compare it to any other taste, yet I knew at once that I was breathing again. My eyelids, sealed shut with dryness, fought hard to fight off the pinkish glow they were now presented with after so long with only blackness to deal with. I felt something take hold of my hand.

'Amazing,' a withered old voice whispered. The first sound I had heard in forever. 'You live.' My hand was let go of and it dropped back to my side. 'I apologise for wakening you from your rest, but I must guarantee my own immortality – my end nears.' This was the last voice I'd heard and was now the first. Suddenly he sobbed uncontrollably. 'I don't want to be frozen like Hobble! I want to be reborn in a new body, just like you Peter.' My eyes slowly opened of their own accord and I saw above me an emancipated old man. His hair, black but greying, and spiky stubble on his cheeks; he let a speck of dribble drop from his chapped lips onto my forehead. Moisture. I was desperate for moisture. I wanted to drown.

'Hitler,' was a word which found its way out of my mouth.

'Open your mind to The Space,' a voice encouraged – not Hitler's, but my own. There I now stood, another me, next to the evil mass murderer above me. 'Everything is nothing. No order, no lies. Deny your anchor, scape the goats.' I couldn't understand myself.

'Now that the cat is out of the bag,' a voice whispered in my mind. It was an altogether new voice, hitherto unheard by anyone ever. I knew this, and also knew who the voice belonged to. It was mine and it was everyone else's too – the voice of the entire Great Collective rolled into one, the voice of all our hate, anger and resentment at what we had seen, done and had done to us. 'You must reap what you have sown,' the voice explained. I looked back at myself and Hitler above me.

'Why?'

'Reaping is collecting, gathering – a collective of great vastness worthy of personal veneration. It is all you have left to gain, to achieve.'

'Reaping what?'

'Revenge, destruction. I am Reaping Icon and the crops are crying out for rain.'

At once I realised the natural conclusion of The Space's gift to humanity, of any gift to humanity – a reaping of ultimate evil. I knew exactly what The Space was – I'd always known. To block It was my only option.

My strength renewed, I threw my being into myself above, leaving the drained shell in the coffin behind. I sealed my old self back in and thrashed Hitler to the floor.

'I beg of you,' he wept.

'Oh boo hoo you bastard!'

My hands found themselves around his neck and I squeezed as hard as I possibly could. His own hands were too weak, too feeble, to do anything but hang like a doll's by his side and shake as my assault grew in ferocity. Soon his shaking stopped and his life left this awful place. I dropped him, straightening my back and looking down at what I had done. I felt rather worthless and cruel – and all the more human. Yet, it simply was not a true occurrence – he remained alive above me and I in my casket as a banging sounded in the distance. 'They are rounding up my escaped subordinates.' He paused, then laughed. 'I died many years ago, just like you Peter Smith – that is the official *story*. They will never capture me.' The banging intensified and yelling sounded in a foreign tongue. I could not make out their words, but anger and jubilance was definitely the tone.

Hitler turned to look in the direction of the noise – laughing again, hysterically, cackling: 'Mossad! I created Israel, gave the Jews a homeland. My legacy, eternal unrest!'

'Lies!' one of the voices shouted, this time in English. 'Our journey home began long before you ever existed.'

'I want to live again, forever, to witness with my own eyes what I have done,' Hitler cried at me, ignoring their words.

I smelt a gust of wind – delicious, stale wind – move across the room above me as shots fired all around and Hitler ducked out of view. A bullet passed through my own shoulder and my side as I summoned up the desire to feel it – it was not forthcoming. Almost at once I was slamming face-first onto the floor, tipped over and left like a beached jellyfish as more shots fired around and into me. Ahead of me I saw Hitler struggling as one end of a rope was tied around his neck whilst the other was thrown over a rafter above his head.

'Ein reich,' he yelled as the men around him jeered and drowned him out, 'ein volk,' he choked out as they hauled him into the air by his neck. His head swelled and his tongue shot out as his body hung there like a caught fish. He was dry, scaly and looked very sad to have had his end brought to him as his side-parting fell over his eyes. He could no longer comb it back.

Now the men turned back to me, but before anything could occur another group burst in and bullets were exchanged. I was picked up and tossed around by the separate gangs as bullets and screams reigned supreme – a cacophony of wasp shrieks. Before I knew it I had a grey hessian sack thrust over my head and my hands bound tightly behind me as I was swiftly moved along and thrown into some kind of vehicle with the engine already running. Soon enough my captors and I were on the move.

It was cold, icily so, and the thought of my senses returning at first gave rise to a euphoria within me before being replaced by utter terror. Where had I been, where was I being taken – and by whom? In a way I just didn't care – I had spent an infinity suffocating in my own coffin only to be let loose and confined once more. Humans were the vilest of the lot, a trumped up beast bent on being an eternal tosser. My anger began to swell and I wriggled in contempt – this landed me an almighty blow to the head.

* * *

The sun woke me up. At least, it felt and looked like the sun. It had been such an age since I'd experienced it that I instantly doubted my self and my senses. I was lying in a huge bed with light brown sheets, almost cream, and could feel every single ache and pain brought down upon me. My head was splitting, my chest was crushing and my wrists were cut and sore. Nevertheless I could move, and move I did. I leapt out of the bed, only to come crashing down straight away. My legs were boney and weak, and I was completely naked. Looking around the room at the high yellow walls, I spotted a black chest of drawers near a door. Pulling myself up and struggling over to it, I opened the top drawer and found the underwear and shirt I needed to conceal my modesty. Once dressed I moved over to a wardrobe against another wall and found in it a single smart brown suit hanging up and a pair of brown shoes to match. I put them on and tried the handle of the door – open. I gently closed it again, staying in the room and walking over to the window. I could see nothing outside but a bright spotlight shining in. There seemed nothing beyond it, either nothing there or nothing worth looking at. I turned back to the door and approached it again, hesitant as to what further pains awaited me outside. At least in here I was alone and it was quiet and trouble-free. For now. Trouble was never far away.

Opening the door wide, I looked out down a long yellow corridor with dozens of doors running along both walls. My options were seemingly limitless and I could not choose which to go through. I carried on walking, right to the end, and now faced the final door – the opposite one to that which I'd exited – turning to look down the long corridor I'd just come down. In a way it felt I'd come up it and not down, though I couldn't decide either way and now chose to open the door I'd reached. It was locked. I waited a moment before knocking on it. Before long I heard a key turning and it opened. Facing me was a man wearing a mask of my face. He was identical in build to me, wearing the same suit.

'Hello,' he said in a foreign accent, outstretching his hand. Instinctively I shook it, and he pulled me into the room, locking the door behind us. The room was identical to the one I'd just come from and my host sat himself down on the bed. I stayed standing, restless, wondering where my life would lead me next. 'You cannot know who I am, but I can help you get home.'

'Home? I have no home,' was my reply. I did not have a home, not one I could remember.

'Back to your home country, to your family home. You have loved ones waiting for your return,' he said encouragingly.

'And why do you want to help me get back there?' I questioned suspiciously, unable to fully engage with a mask of my face. The eyes were cut out so that he could see from behind it, but the holes were too small to allow me to actually see *his* eyes. I didn't want to see them – suddenly I wanted what he offered me, a home and a family to return to. There was somebody, somewhere, waiting for me to come home. My cheeks felt moist, so I rubbed them. There were tears coming from my eyes. How strange. What a peculiar thing for me to do.

'You have suffered enough at the hands of a monstrous man, you must retire to a life of home comforts and relaxation.'

'Wouldn't the human instinct be to keep me hidden here from the world? Hitler said the world thought he was dead long before he actually was; if that's true, I know too much. I am better off dead.'

'Trust me,' the man laughed, 'we have tried to kill you, but you simply recover. You are the indestructible man. We fear you and your powers.'

I narrowed my eyes, rubbing at my stiff neck. I could feel a scar just below my right ear and I followed its course across my neck with my fingers right up to my left ear. Nor had I died in my sealed tomb, where no oxygen could penetrate. I was surely immortal.

'Who slit my throat?' I growled at the man, suddenly feeling that anger was justified.

'One of our men,' he answered casually. 'I put four bullets in the back of your head.'

I charged at him, pulling him up off the bed. 'By the time I've finished with you, you'll regret every single breath you've ever drawn into your sorry little lungs,' I shouted as I threw him against the wardrobe. The force broke the doors and sent him inside it momentarily, before he came tumbling back out with a thud.

'The fact you'll finish is victory for me – an end, finitude,' he said calmly back. The mask of my face had slipped off, revealing the very pale, haggard face of a man in his fifties who had obviously worked hard beyond his years. He looked resigned to whatever fate was forthcoming, and I now controlled that fate. I paused my assault, staring down as he looked back up and forced a smile. 'They threatened to murder my wife and child, so I joined their cause. They murdered them anyway. I grew accustomed to the brutality, accepted the atrocities around me and became a part of them.'

'You shot me.'

'You were unconscious, an easy target. I didn't know who you were, and I still don't, but you survived. I have shot many people before, but you are the first to live. That has wakened me up to the crimes I have committed.' His smile had vanished, and his face had turned ashen. 'I was told it was in the name of my country, in the name of defeating our enemies. Here you are before me, a real person – you are a human being.'

'Yet I cannot die?'

'We will never stamp out our enemies, because in reality we have no enemies – we humans just have each other.' I outstretched my hand to his and helped him to his feet. 'You will return to your country and have your life,' he finished.

* * *

There had been no family waiting for me – they were all dead. There was nothing, save for perhaps everything – a beginning. I could start anew, have my life over. It was now 1961 and I was only thirty-six. I could put aside my past and move on, making a life for myself in the long future ahead. But, did I really want to?

I'd never been used to having friends and, quite frankly, didn't really want any. They were a burden and a tie, leeching off any potential good nature within me. Truthfully, there wasn't much good nature – the horrors

Hitler had subjected me to had seen off any sympathy I may have possessed for the human race. I now viewed what I was living as an apathetic sentience; knowing how low humanity sinks on a daily basis but having no ability, or want, to alter it. I felt I outgrew people, moved on from them and onto the next. Oh how self-indulgent to feel myself standing away from the crowd and being an individual – something all of them felt they were doing too. There's nothing different about me, nothing different about any of us. We're all the same, all here just existing and thinking that we're thinking. All that, of course, went out the window somewhat when I met Gary and Sarah Noose. I felt an overwhelming pulse of purity permeating through their being – they were as one unit entirely; completely devoted to each other and beholden of a clean aura. It is difficult to explain fully, but when I looked at, or even just thought about them, I could see a clarity so transparently that it shot me in the stomach. The pain was a drug, a yearning for all of humanity to be the way they were.

It was entirely by chance that our paths crossed. I would often walk alone in Myrtle Forest, vague moments of déjà vu taking me back to some lost childhood centuries ago as Mother pursued me playfully through the long grassy growth. It seemed rubbish and the truth in equal measure, especially when I came across a water well right in the middle of the forest – quite a queer place for one – and there, crouching the other side of it, were Gary and Sarah. Had I seen them at a distance I'd have scarpered in the opposite direction, but now that I was so close I had to interact.

'Good day,' I said to them, looking down the well. I could see myself jumping in. It was the perfect method of dashing away from this place. They'd probably fish me out.

'Hello there,' the man replied, getting up. 'I'm Gary Noose, and this is my wife Sarah.' He held out his hand to shake mine. I obliged. His was a firm workers hand, wrought with rough yet moist skin. He looked about my age, mid thirties – perhaps a little younger, and his black hair was thinning on top. He stood tall and slim, a very smart man, with a healthy complexion.

'I'm Peter, Peter Smith.' I moved to have a look at Sarah, who remained on the ground. She was sitting on a tartan blanket with a picnic basket between her legs. I could see she was pregnant, her swollen belly sitting proudly there. She was wearing a loose-fitting flowery dress and had her brown hair tied back. They were both so ordinary and so beautiful that I felt at once drawn to them.

'We're having a picnic, care to join us?' Sarah asked.

'I'd love to,' said I, the words escaping my mouth before I could do anything about it. 'If I'm not intruding, that is?' Pray I was not. I could not leave now. Queer that I should wish to turn to prayer to fulfil my desire, yet it seemed the logical option – unabated wishful thinking right this second.

'Of course not,' Gary comforted, encouraging me to sit down as he did. I did so, easing myself slowly down across from them.

'Are you local?' I decided to ask them, forcing idle chit chat. It did not feel natural to me, but I felt I wanted to continue.

'Yes, we live in Myrtleville,' Gary answered. 'How about you?'

'I was born here, and spent my youth here. The war took me abroad, but I'm back now.'

'Such a devastating war,' Sarah sighed.

'I stayed here throughout, trained as a police officer,' Gary explained.

'Not an easy job,' I tried to brown-nose, 'but a rewarding one.'

'Yes, it is.'

It was now I realised Gary seemed overly relaxed and accepting of me and my sudden presence, despite him being an officer of the law. My preconception would have assumed his skepticism and suspicion at my wandering alone in the forest.

'I'm just in love with this wishing well,' Sarah gushed, holding her stomach as she turned a little to look it up and down. 'Do you know, I've lived here my whole life and this is the first time I've ever seen it. I could have sworn I've been this way as a child, yet I never saw it before.'

'Well it's certainly not a new well, darling,' Gary pointed out, rubbing a finger along the rough stone as bits of the age-old lichen broke away into dust and blew away in the slight breeze.

Some particles got in my nostrils, and I knew I'd smelt that scent before – I saw my mother chasing after me, hundreds of years prior, as I sought to hide this place from her. Something awful had happened to her and I, just a child, had sought out suicide as my solace. The well had saved me, somehow, but that remained yet hazy in my mind. Now my well was exposed, discovered by this couple and their unborn child. Perhaps this was the family I had returned home for? Sarah giggled a little and the couple kissed briefly. They were so wonderful.

I stayed with them another hour or more, waxing lyrical about my trouble with Hitler and the unexpected occurrence of Thaddeus Hobble. They didn't believe a word of it, of course, but found my story ever so entertaining and, more importantly, me charming.

'We really must be heading off,' Gary eventually announced as Sarah began to feel weary.

'I'm more than eight months gone – not long now,' Sarah added, getting to her feet with the help of her doting husband.

I sensed I had outstayed my welcome somewhat, so said my goodbyes and left them to it.

* * *

That night I tossed and turned in my little bed in the bedsit, not a window to look out but four dark green walls to hide the outside from view. I thought of nothing else but Gary and Sarah Noose, the summation of everything possibly good in mankind. I wondered if I'd ever see them again, and in a way hoped I wouldn't – to leave it at that, with them high on a pedestal of perfection, was enough for me. Were fate to steer their lives towards mine, then I would certainly go with it and allow a lasting friendship to occur. The rest of my life would be very lonely without good people to populate it. There was nobody more good than them.

Eventually I rolled over and managed to struggle into sleep. There, I was bombarded with colliding visions of multiple me's, all vying for my attention. They *were* me, I knew it, but some had different names and different faces as well as the duplicates. I was all these people and more, and they all cried out something different, draining each other out. I could not make out any of it. Suddenly they all ceased, turning their backs to me and pulling up a hood over their heads. When they turned back their faces – my faces – were concealed and the hellish din did not return. One single figure emerged from within them, a tall thin blonde woman with her hair obscuring her features and a long greyish white dress dragging on the floor. Yet, there *was* no floor for it to drag on. No floor I could see. She was not me, yet she seemed familiar and distant – someone I should have known but couldn't remember, or perhaps I had yet to meet. I called her towards me, asking to see her face. She neared only minutely, stopping and pausing as I sensed I should now move closer to her. I could not, I was fixed and useless. Then, I fell backwards and woke up covered in sweat. I got up and dressed, I would not sleep again tonight.

* * *

Early the next morning I took a stroll around the village, deciding to head into town to look for some more permanent employment than odd jobs and gardening. On my way I passed the police station, stopping outside and wondering for a brief moment whether or not to go in and see if Gary Noose was on duty. No, that would not endear me to him – to hassle him at work would be detrimental to any potential friendship ahead. Just that second a police car pulled up alongside me and Gary himself stuck his head out.

'Get in,' he called out.

'Hello there,' I replied.

'Get in,' he repeated, snappier this time. His tone was completely different from yesterday. I obliged, jumping in the passenger seat and shutting the door just in time for him to speed off down the road. 'It was easier than I thought it would be,' he suddenly said.

'What was?'

'Finding you, Peter. I imagined driving around town all day or traipsing the forest again to try and spot you.' He wiped the sweat off his brow, briefly flicking his eyes to look in the rear view mirror. 'Chance, or fate, brought you right to me.'

'What's this all about?'

He pulled over in a lay-by and burst into tears. I wanted to put my arm around his shoulder to offer my support, and nearly did – but something just held me back, some emotionally apathetic shield crippling my joints.

'I'm just so weak right now, Peter, and this isn't like me,' he sobbed like a child.

'What do you mean, weak?'

'It's the baby coming, I guess.' He pulled a hanky from his breast pocket and blew his nose, his tears easing. 'I feel I can turn to you, confide in you. We're very similar, you and me.'

I felt honoured and terrified at this opinion of his. 'Go on, Gary,' I uttered, my arm still unable to reach out to him. Perhaps I could do that verbally instead.

'I love Sarah so much, and now she's going to make me a father, a daddy.'

'You'll make a great father,' I encouraged, thinking it the right thing to do. Equally, I could think of nothing else to say and couldn't quite understand the predicament he felt he was in. Perhaps his tears were jubilation, or panic?

'Thank you, my friend,' he replied with a warm smile, reaching out to shake my hand. We stayed silent, holding hands for a minute or more as I felt his blood pressure easing. 'You must come and visit Sarah and me at our home,' he went on, giving me his address. It was an open invitation.

After this he was as he had been the day before. His opening up to me made him even more perfect and complete.

* * *

That evening, as the sun had gone and I strolled along the countryside away from Myrtleville town, I spotted a car parked up between the trees – it was Gary's. For a moment I was pleased, then worried, and finally suspicious. I approached the vehicle slowly. The windows were steaming up and it was rocking from side to side. As I neared I could see Gary's bare bottom going up and down, two well-shaven female legs either side of it wrapping around. She was a blonde, her skirt still on but pushed up and her small breasts bobbing as Gary's thrusts intensified. With the passenger seat wound all the way back, Gary had all the space he needed to commit his infidelity. I pulled away, devastated, dashing away before I was seen.

I didn't know what to do, but eventually found myself at Gary and Sarah's house. Knocking on the door, I got no answer. As the strain I was under intensified, I tried the handle and it was open – I stepped inside without a moment's thought and called out for Sarah.

'Gary?' she screamed out from upstairs. I dashed up them, following her voice.

'It's me, Peter,' I shouted back, entering the bedroom where she lay sprawled on the bed with her bare legs spread apart. The sweat was absolutely raining off her and she kept on screaming out in pain. The bed was soaking.

'The baby's come early,' she cried out through her deep breaths.

'Oh God!' I blurted out, the sweat now pouring off me as well. I neared, peering between her legs as a tiny little head was making its way from within her. Instinctively I put my hands down there and supported the tiny little body as it kept on coming. 'Push,' I called out to her, not knowing what else to say. 'Push!'

'I am!' she yelled back.

Suddenly the baby was out. 'It's a boy,' I cried, the tears streaming down my face.

'A son,' she sobbed. 'My son Henry Noose.'

As I knelt there holding her baby, I felt myself come over all queer. I looked ahead and the wall behind her bed had fallen away. There was now a large black box, standing upright. A very slim, very pale blonde woman seemed to be with it, but her face was covered by her long hair – she was the one from my dream. I slumped back, stumbling to the floor and slamming against the wall behind me. I looked down, the baby still in my arms and its umbilical cord stretched out and still attached to Sarah. I felt myself dying – I knew I was dying – and the last intake of air to enter my lungs occurred. Gary appeared at the door as my vision darkened then extinguished altogether. I was dead.

A SIMPLE EXPLANATION FOR ANTHONY THE SILENT

In every young person's life there comes the realisation that the world is not as clear cut as Mother and Father had painted it. Usually this happens at school, when mixing with contemporaries. Child's simple cosseted ideals are swiftly washed away in a swathe of pack mentality. For Little Tony, however, it came about in a most unexpected place and way.

Little Tony wasn't short – far from it. He was rather tall for his meagre seven years, and not thin, and he'd never been to school. In fact, Little Tony had never left the house. He was Little Tony because of his intelligence. It was low. So low, in fact, that his parents deemed it inappropriate to educate him at all. He would be much better served by isolation, they decided, and so the boy found himself constantly present in just a single room. A bucket for his waste, and his meals thrust through a hatch at the bottom of the door, Little Tony knew nothing of the outside world. If truth be told, it could be said he didn't want to know. He was happy to wee and poo both in (and quite often around) his bucket, and feast upon the scraps Mother and Father shoved through the hatch. So contented was Little Tony, that he could occupy his time entirely free from thought. He knew no different, and having no access to any stimulation other than his own flat mind alleviated him from resentment. His parents weren't his captors, they were just unseen deliverers of sustenance. Little Tony never even gave any thought as to how his bucket got emptied. It just did. One minute he'd be feeling sleepy, the next he'd wake up and his room was clean. It *was* his room, but he didn't feel possessive over it. There was simply no need to feel possessive. He'd never had any interaction with anyone, not even his own parents above a superficial level, and so knew nothing of possession. He knew nothing of anything, except that he pissed and shat in the bucket and ate from the tray shoved through the hatch. That was his entire world.

Life wasn't slow in Little Tony's room. It wasn't quick either. Time just didn't exist at all. There were no windows to ascertain day and night; only the single bulb dangling from the ceiling did that. When it went out, the boy felt sleepy and then he woke up when it came back on. He didn't think anything of sleep, it was just something that happened. It was neither bad nor good, it was just an occurrence like the bucket and the food tray. There was nothing else apart from these in the room, save for the rug he slept on. Now that could have been instinct – using it to sleep on – for Little Tony could possibly sense that it felt more comfortable than the bare floorboards. Not that he knew what a rug or floorboards were. He didn't want to know either; he was quite happy existing in blissful ignorance. There he would lay, on the rug that was possibly his – though he found no need to insist on ownership over it – staring up at the yellow ceiling. The light only ever cast the same circle-shaped shadow on it – never moving, never relenting its presence. He would stare up at it, not much thought going through his head. He never had a care in the world (or room) to trouble him. His food would always arrive, the bucket would always get emptied and the light would always go off and come back on again. Mother and

Father were the other side of the door, and Little Tony seemed to know this. That was their life, and this was his. Nothing had ever happened to shatter that. And then one day, his food tray did not arrive.

At first, the boy was not concerned. Concern had never been a concern of his. And, time did not exist here. But, as the period of the tray of food not appearing extended, Little Tony began to feel like he needed the food. This new sensation grew and grew, the concept of time beginning to show glimpses of formation in the boy's head. After two days, the contents of the bucket were looking decidedly enticing and Little Tony was forced to consume them. Instinct registered – this was not a good idea. But, it was his only idea. Rather quickly it made him feel even worse than before. His bubble had been well and truly burst. Suddenly half of him felt really awful, whilst the other half felt like he'd just been born this very second. All at once he knew stuff – in the sense that he was aware there were actual emotions. He sensed desire, anger, abandonment. The door now looked like it led somewhere else, away from this awful place. Little Tony now wanted to be away from this room – only briefly – then he just wanted things to go back to how they were before. The sheer horror of having to change things didn't bear thinking about. Surely Mother and Father would just start up the old routine again? That was the best possible outcome, the boy felt. This was all new to him, all these ideas and feelings, and he wasn't too fond of them.

Suddenly the door opened. It was the first time Little Tony had actually seen it opening for himself, though by now he had reasoned that that is what it did. In stepped a strange figure in a strange uniform. 'Anthony,' he called out as he just stood there looking at him. 'My name is Henry Noose, and I'm from the police. Are you okay, Anthony?'

* * *

'An aberration,' Inspector Hastings announced – both vaguely and stoically – as he strode through the grey corridor leading to his office in Myrtleville police station. He opened the office door and briefly paused to look back at Sergeant Noose.

'Horrific – keeping a child prisoner since birth. One of the worst cases I've worked on,' Noose replied.

'Not that, my medical,' Hastings snapped back. The younger man studied his superior's prematurely white hair and reddened complexion. 'I investigate crimes, not chase after drugged-up youths. I shouldn't need to be as fit as a butcher's dog!'

'It does help if you're healthy though, Sir,' Noose cautiously uttered. With a big sigh, Hastings vanished and slammed the door behind him. Noose turned and bumped into Peter Smith. The young teen dropped the papers he was carrying and promptly fumbled to pick them all up again. 'Who are you, what are you doing in the station?'

'Sorry, I'm after Inspector Hastings,' the boy coyly replied, gathering his papers and trying to move on. Noose stepped in his way.

'I'm Sergeant Henry Noose, I can deal with whatever you want.'

'No,' Peter chuckled, 'I need to speak to an inspector – not his tea boy.' Suddenly Peter realised he'd overstepped the mark, and he hadn't been able to help himself. Noose's face was ashen with rage. 'I'm in my last year at school and want to do my work experience here,' he blurted out, smiling.

Noose raised an eyebrow. 'I see.'

'I have an urge to solve mysteries – like I can sense

there's unknowns to be uncovered,' the boy went on, again dropping his papers. This time, he did not bend to pick them up. He became transfixed on Noose's face - a very ordinary, longish face. Thin brownish hair lay atop the head, already beginning to vacate it slowly as a small bald patch fought for living space. He was tall, but round-shouldered, and hadn't shaved this morning. He was not unlike Peter Smith in looks, although Peter had yet to begin shaving.

'What are you looking at?' Noose demanded of this weird lad.

'You.'

'Why, is there something on my face?'

Peter thought about Noose's face and decided it wasn't the face he was looking at at all; it was the man himself. The essence, the being. Startled, he turned and dashed away. The sergeant picked up the boy's papers and briefly flicked through them. They were just stories - crime stories - scrawled in pencil on the crumpled paper.

* * *

'Isn't it beautiful?' Noose called out as he came to stand next to Peter.

'What is?' the teenager asked the slightly older man, keeping his gaze fixed ahead at Myrtle Forest in the valley below and the Welsh mountains behind it.

'The world - all this,' Noose went on, waving his hand around at the view. The late afternoon sun was just disappearing behind the mountains and the greeny golden trees were in shadow.

'I guess.' He had sprinted from the police station at first, but soon found himself arrested by the view in the distance. The trees were beautiful, yes - what was left of them. Many had been felled for housing developments. Lots and lots of people. Buzz buzz buzzing.

'The world is a wondrous place, lad,' Noose went on, 'full of simple joyousness – if you look at things in the right way.' He held up Peter's papers. 'There are some bad people, who do bad things. The good people have a framework set in place to try and stop them. Sometimes it works, sometimes it doesn't – but there *are* good people. Maybe your stories would benefit from following a similar moral model.' He handed them back. Peter folded them up and stuffed them in his back trouser pocket.

'You read some of my stuff?'

'I saw some line about humanity being sick and evil.'

'You say there are some good people,' Peter pondered, 'but what is good?'

'You're so young to be so cynical,' Noose sighed. 'I bet you've done nothing in your life yet. You haven't lived.' The sergeant turned to leave, pausing and putting a hand on Peter's shoulder. 'And please, stay away from the station. Go and find work experience somewhere else.' With this, he walked off.

* * *

'Their daughter Kelly is already in care,' Hastings yelled down the phone, 'how the hell did this brother Tony of hers slip through the net? They kept him locked up like a bloody dog!'

Noose was standing the other side of his superior's desk. He briefly eyed up the fish tank dumped on top of several filing cabinets. There was water in it, and bubbles pumping around, but no fish. Hastings slammed the phone down and leapt up, storming over to the cabinets. He yanked one of the drawers open and grabbed hold of some fish food.

'It's a horrible case of child abuse,' Noose said almost nonchalantly.

'You *will* see good in people, won't you boy?' Hastings grunted back, lifting the lid on the fish tank and sprinkling some food on top of the water. Noose stared blankly back, having witnessed this ritual for months now. There were no fish to miraculously appear and consume the food. 'You'll come a cropper one day.'

'What do you mean by that, *Sir?*' Noose gingerly questioned.

'Horrible case? I can tell by the way you say things – horrible fucking case? It's downright depraved. The human race is a vile speck of shit under the sole of the universe's shoe.' Tears almost welled in his eyes, but not quite. 'The things I've seen.'

'I've seen some pretty awful things too, but I still try to stay positive. There's a lot of good out there,' was Noose's response. A sceptical Hastings turned to face his sergeant – more to ensure his raised eyebrow had been witnessed than anything else.

'How's the family – your little boy?' Hastings suddenly asked, changing the subject.

'Super, thanks.' Noose smiled as widely as he could. 'Growing up fast.'

'Yes,' Hastings replied vaguely, tapping his chin as he went about adding more food to the fish tank.

Noose's thoughts were filled with Tony and Peter. He somehow imagined them as the same person, or at the very least composites of some whole. The sergeant had shown a remarkable ability to pigeon-hole these things – these crimes he investigated. Peter wasn't a part of any crime he was involved with, but he was a part of the overall spectrum of goings-on at the station. He and Tony had come to his attention on the same day, thus they were in the same section in Noose's mind. They were one and the same – neither had seen or done anything yet in their short lives. Noose was certain of that. They'd been held back for different reasons, but held back nonetheless. Tony's bind was physical – an actual locked door. Peter's, Noose reasoned, was partly physical owing to his youth but largely mental – his outlook was tainting and halting potential experiences.

* * *

'Hello Peter,' said his best friend David. Peter just smiled back, briefly, as David kept looking at his eyes and lips.

Suddenly Peter's younger brother Stuart – all a bright flop of blonde hair and deep cobalt eyes – dashed past in the school yard with a gang of other boys. 'Get a room, bum boys,' he yelled at his brother and his friend as half the children on the yard burst into fits of laughter. Peter's face reddened as he gritted his teeth, but David hadn't appeared to have heard the comment. His features, positioned in the centre of a chubby round face, remained fixed and almost trancelike.

'Don't listen to them,' he suddenly said, Stuart's words obviously having registered with him. 'We can be who we want to be.'

'What do you mean?' Peter interrogated.

David broke eye contact, wandering off. 'Oh, never mind,' he mumbled as he went.

Just now the snootiest girl in school strutted past – Lucy Davies. Short, with an hourglass figure and sporting a face full of makeup, she swished her long dark hair away from her face and gossiped with her friends. Peter just stood and watched, transfixed on her as David had been on him. She didn't acknowledge his existence. He hadn't even registered in her peripheral vision. He wasn't quite sure what he'd do with her, but he knew it happened in the bedroom and that she'd have to enjoy it. Now his mind was filled with David, who had stopped in the distance and was looking back at Peter.

* * *

That evening the two lads went walking in Myrtle Forest. David wished to keep on going deeper and deeper in, moving further and further away from the main path. Peter went to turn back, a bizarre dizziness and visions of a water well overwhelming him. David grabbed his hand and pulled him – the pair fell over, David ending up on top. He gazed intently into Peter's eyes, suddenly kissing him on the lips. In an instant Reaping Icon appeared above the pair.

'Peter Smith – so many pasts and so many futures,' said the one who looked like a man, but could not be seen. 'You are trapped, I have halted you. You are mine to meddle with.'

Against the backdrop of empty existence dangled Darren, Stuart, Jim and Anthony too, like wet knickers on a whirligig – fit only for Reaping Icon's games. He had come from them, and now controlled them. He grabbed Peter now and tossed him along his timeline, fiddling and toying wherever he so wished.

DO NOT ADJUST YOUR SEX

All women were extinct. Even so, David seemed overly eager to enter into a homosexual relationship with me.

'Needs must,' he quipped, casually unbuttoning his shirt. I was not ready. Still in my mind were the women, mostly agreeable, who had since perished. I surveyed the listless grey sea ahead of us. Mankind was now arid, though Nature had neglected to notice. It went on regardless of humanity's latest problem, all other female species surviving intact. I had a girlfriend in the old world, before all the women went. We'd never had sex, but I knew I wasn't gay – I just *knew*.

I looked over at David's exposed, hairless chest as he sat himself down on the rock. It was not unpleasant and I'd seen it before – he'd always been my best mate. Even after I found out he was gay in sixth form, we remained close friends. His sexuality had never troubled me because I felt so secure in my own. I fancied women, and I'd always wanted to have sex with women. This, of course, had never happened for me because my girlfriend Lucy had been quite shy. I was shy too, in a way, and just hadn't seized the opportunity. Now that the virus had wiped her and her fellow females out, I would never get the opportunity to have heterosexual intercourse.

'I can't do it,' I told David, turning and walking away. He got up and rushed to me, taking my hand and yanking it to stop me in my tracks.

'If you want to lose your virginity, then why not lose it with me?' he said quite sensibly. He had a point. 'Your only other option is a bloody animal or something.'

I didn't want to have to do that. I looked again at his chest, keeping away from his eyes. They had always been my friend's eyes, not my lover's. Would one session of sex, just to get it out of the way, really make him my lover? Would it even be proper sex? I didn't know anything about gay sex – I hadn't a clue. To be honest, I hadn't a clue about straight sex either. The whole spectrum of sex had eluded me. I knew David had done it before, because he always told me about his conquests. He oozed confidence and experience. It didn't trouble me to hear the details of his exploits, and I wasn't sickened by the two men thing. My mother didn't like it, though, and she'd always encouraged me to stay away from David and "his ilk", as she put it. Well, she was gone with the rest of them now. Really, it seemed as though only David and I remained in the whole of the world. It could have been the case this warm summer evening as we stood alone together on the beach.

'I'm not sure I *can* have gay sex, let alone with you,' I uttered.

'Why not?' he asked me straight out.

'I don't know.'

'Well I'm not going to force you, but the offer is there.' I looked back at his face and he was smiling warmly. He wasn't an unattractive man by any means – not that I could really tell if a man was attractive or not. I found women attractive. David's smooth chest – at least, it looked smooth – was just like a woman's, except he had no breasts. He did have nipples though, and these were probably the next best thing. I was never a breast man anyway. I felt myself compelled to feel his chest to see if it really was as smooth as it looked. Instinctively, though awkwardly, I moved the hand David was holding towards his chest. He brought it the final few inches, pressing it against his heartbeat. I felt a rush of pain down my spine, my mind filled with Lucy and her beautiful jet-black hair. But, she was gone now and David was right here in front of me.

I pulled my hand off his chest and stayed still, several thoughts now dashing through my mind. Was I averse to what could happen between the two of us because it was with another man, or because he was doing the chasing? With Lucy, the thrill had been in her seeming reluctance and my pursuing of her. It had spurred me on, made me desperate to be with her. Now, here with David, it was a completely different circumstance. He stepped closer to me and, as though he was leaning in for a kiss, just gave me a friendly hug. I was strangely disappointed for a flash, wishing he *had* kissed me. Why hadn't he kissed me? As he pulled away, his arms still around me, I lost all control of myself and kissed him on the lips. Now it was his turn to step back from me.

'Do you want this or not?' he asked.

'Do I have a choice?'

'There is always a choice with intimacy, nobody can force you into anything.'

I wasn't sure what other choice there was left to me, but my body seemed to be making the decision as I got that shortness of breath before an erection. I tried to conceal it, turning away from him as my penis hardened in my trousers. It was very difficult to hide, and David stepped up close to put his hand down there. I jolted him, which he didn't find surprising.

'I'm uneasy,' I told him. 'I've never been inclined towards this sort of thing.'

'I will always be here for you, you are my best friend and always will be,' he replied. Maybe that was the problem? That this offer would always be there made me less inclined to seize the opportunity now. I'd always thought Lucy would be there, and hadn't rushed with her. Perhaps David would not always be here after all? To seize the day, to do this with him today whilst my emotions were so high and so penetrating, would be to make that crucial step I had not yet taken in life. Why put it off any longer? There was nothing stopping me now.

I had never felt these urges before, and yet I had never felt repulsion from the idea. Of course I had given it thought, I must have with David speaking about his experiences, but I hadn't desired to partake. Then again, why were there these barriers – these separations and labels – making what I wanted from life different from what David wanted? We were just the same, just human beings here on Earth together right now at this very moment in time. I thought again of all the women who'd been wiped out, and wondered if I should even allow myself to seek happiness. Suicide had become very common since the extinction; some men just couldn't cope. I didn't want to die, especially by my own hand. It seemed monstrous for that to be my legacy in the face of this challenge now facing us as a species. I not only wanted to live, but *needed* to live for all those who had been wiped out. Could I come to represent all the women who had perished by the cruel hand of a freak virus? Would becoming gay bring me closer to this aim? Such a thought in itself disturbed me. People couldn't just become gay, David was proof of that. I'd witnessed his entire life side by side with my own as he struggled to be accepted because of his born sexuality. I quite clearly realised he would never have chosen that. Now, here he was in a world without women, and he didn't seem to mind. Well, he was always good at hiding things so maybe he was concealing his true feelings on the matter.

He certainly seemed to have been hiding his true feelings for me all these years.

'You would not choose to be gay,' I told him.

'Nor would you,' he replied.

'Under normal circumstances,' I mumbled to myself. He had heard me, but did not reply. I was confused why he had even suggested we get together, unless he had seen in me some hint of homosexuality throughout our long friendship. And this was the most confusing angle of all, the fact that we had been such close friends all this time. Was my love as a friend for him muddying the situation? Perhaps my erection just now was a hazy overspill of our deep companionship, and not sexual lust. We had certainly been close all our lives and were both letting ourselves get carried away as emotions ran high. The sheer devastation of what had befallen humankind was difficult to fully absorb. It seemed like a sick practical joke from a higher being, or punishment for unknown crimes. I certainly felt responsible somehow, like I had personally killed every single one of the billions of women who had suffered and died as the virus had spread across the globe. If I was personally to blame, was it then a test to see how I would cope? Was David, in front of me now with his offer of sexual fulfilment, some kind of snake tempting me to take the apple? It did feel like I *would* experience sexual fulfilment, and this was the worrying point. No matter which way I looked at and analysed it in my mind, intimacy on any level with David did not seem wrong – it was the logical step, the absolute right thing to do. But, there was that niggle at the back of my mind that kept whispering "No". The whisper – that faintest of voices struggling to be heard in the incessant cacophony of screeching that was my mind – could easily have been the last residual sound of Lucy as she faded ever more from this sorry excuse for a world. No,

Nature was still glorious and rich in all its diversity; it was humanity that was the sorrow here.

* * *

'It's a shame it took the death of every woman on Earth to bring us together, but I'm glad it did,' David whispered to me as we lay there naked. His hand rested on my chest and his leg was wrapped around mine. 'I always loved you as more than a friend,' he said, his entire being melting on me in such bliss. To this, I could not reply. I didn't know how to. The sex itself had been passionate and not altogether unenjoyable, but I just couldn't stop thinking about Lucy and women in general. I felt I had somehow wronged both them and David, and moved away from him to sit up on the side of the bed. 'What's the matter?' he asked comfortingly, placing his hand on my shoulder. I wanted to shrug it off, but didn't want to upset him. Somehow I owed him; I'd toyed with his emotions, fulfilled his desire and played him like I cared. I did and I didn't care. In the midst of the passion, as he let me bury myself deep into his moist body, I loved him and cared so much. I could still smell that wet odour. Now, I just didn't know.

'I just don't know what to do anymore,' I told him in all honesty. I owed him that much. 'The world is such a mess.'

'There's nothing we can do about it,' he replied, caressing my back with his stubbly chubby chin. There were no opposite sexes now – just men, just David and me. One of his stubbly spikes caught me sharply and I flinched. 'Sorry,' he whispered, his head coming to rest on my shoulder as he ran his hand through my hair, 'my darling.'

I couldn't cope with this and leapt up away from him, bolting out of the room. He didn't follow as I darted into the bathroom and locked the door, desperate to get in the shower.

* * *

Later on he came downstairs as I was on the sofa watching TV. Not many programmes ran now, except for repeats. The news did, however, and was about scientists setting in motion the manufacturing of human babies. They had failed to find a cure for the virus, so I wasn't holding my breath about this latest endeavour. The grotesque mutants they might create didn't bear thinking about. I switched channels as David sat down in the armchair across from me. I kept my eyes fixed on the screen as the Prime Minister delivered one of his numerous speeches on yet another news bulletin: 'This is a divine sign from God,' he went on as he held the Chancellor of the Exchequer's hand, 'being gay is the right thing. For too long we have been a secular nation. Now, as we all question the devastation that has hit the human race and seek answers for our loss, there may be some good to come out of the horror.'

I was wracked with guilt, like I'd cheated on Lucy. To me she was still alive, and at this moment in time she always would be. I got that terrible ache in the pit of my stomach, an overwhelming feeling of hopelessness and dread. David got up and came to sit next to me. He could see I was stiff and uneasy in his presence; strong in my mind was the intimacy we had just shared. The passion had kicked in, we had just lost ourselves and gone with it. Now, I wasn't so sure it was what I wanted.

'You okay?' he asked gently, taking hold of my hand. I thought about pulling away, but by the time I'd thought about it too much time had passed to do so. 'Look, I know this isn't ideal, but it's all we have right now. Let's make the most of it.'

I switched the TV off and turned to him. He was so sincere, so warm. I thought about how warm his body had been in bed; the sweat lubricating as our bodies pressed together. 'You're right,' I whispered, almost not wanting him to hear me. I didn't feel gay – I didn't feel like any sexual orientation – I just wanted to feel myself. There was a sense that I'd never truly felt or been myself yet in life, and now I wondered if this was the turning point in finding out who I really was. The doorbell rang. It never rang these days. Nobody called around anymore. David and I looked at each other, he looking like he wished to prolong this moment with me for as long as possible. The doorbell rang again. He waited, still staring at me but now with a creased brow. I got up and walked into the hallway to the front door. Opening it, I was greeted by a large gathering of people. One man held a film camera in my face whilst another stood just to his side with a boom mic. Then, a beautiful young woman in a short glittery red dress stepped forward and began speaking directly into the camera:

'And here we are with the man himself, as we reveal the experiment to him and bring him back from under hypnosis.'

'I, I,' I stuttered, gawping at the woman. A woman, alive! It was unreal and yet completely natural and right at the same time. 'What's going on?'

'Uterus,' she replied, and instantly I felt my head split like an axe had sliced it open. I could remember everything, this was just a reality TV show that I had agreed to be hypnotised on. How foolish I had been. All the women of Earth weren't dead at all, it was all a cheap trick for entertainment that I'd been paid to partake in. It wasn't real at all. I could feel my flaccid, curled penis throbbing with torture in my pants. I had had sex with David – that was real. Lucy! She was alive. I wished I could just slit my own throat right that second, but I didn't have the guts. All I had was the shame to smile into the camera and wonder why I'd ever agreed to take part in this in the first place.

* * *

I didn't want to face Lucy. I didn't want to face anyone. My own mother had seen the whole thing happen with her own eyes – my fall into the abyss. There was a studio set up ready to interview me, ready to pry into my innermost feelings on the event, but I just wanted to die. Alone now for the briefest of moments as the live interview was being prepared during the ad break, I stared at myself in the dressing room mirror. Was the reflection even mine? It looked ghastly and inhuman, perverted beyond the depths of depravity. How could I have agreed to take part in this show? I'd been so confident about it, so in need of external attention. The hunger for instant fame had blocked the reality from my mind. I'd been shy and nervous, yes; so why had I plucked up the courage to put myself in such a position? But then I thought of David… and I wanted him. Suddenly I felt myself tugged away from this place and cast down elsewhere.

* * *

Stuart was sitting across from me at the breakfast table, grinning just a little too much. I don't know what he had to grin about. Was the prospect of a day of school ahead of him cause for such mirth? Being that little bit younger than me, he still had a yard's length to go before finishing his educational stint, but somehow I felt less advanced than he.

145

That grin was all it took to make me feel he knew something I didn't, or had done something I hadn't. It took me all my strength not to yell at him and cause a scene. But, I wouldn't let him have that.

'What are you plans for the day, Peter?' he suddenly asked me in a sly tone.

'Yes, Peter, what *are* your plans for the day?' Mother rounded, squaring her eyes at mine as she joined us at the table with a slice of toast slathered in marmalade.

'I have important work to undertake down at the police station,' said I, deciding to at least attempt some sort of fabrication.

'What important work?' Stuart carried on, that nasty glint in his eye as the morning sun caught his bright blonde hair. I ducked away, surprised by its intensity.

'Speak up,' Mother roared. 'Another day of fannying around, is it?' She took in a mouthful of toast, and carried on talking: 'You need a job, Peter, not this obsession with solving local mysteries.'

'But, I feel drawn to it, Mother,' I cut in gingerly, shielding my face from the onslaught of moist toast shards shooting from her open mouth. Stuart giggled. 'I feel the need to solve crimes.'

'Rubbish! You're wasting your life, Peter. You need a job, not a passion. You don't want to end up one of these middle-aged losers living on welfare at home with their mothers, do you?'

I felt rather broken by this. Still, it was nothing new. I'd heard the same thing day in day out since finishing school, and Stuart knew exactly how to initiate such diatribes. That was how we left the discussion, for soon enough I had finished my own breakfast and headed out on my bicycle to Myrtleville police station. There, I knew I would find, amongst other interesting things, Lucy Davies. Short, dark-haired and round-bottomed, she was a sight almost too overbearing to look at. If you stared for too long, it would result in the extermination of your sight – nothing more would you wish to look upon, as you'd have already seen it all. We had very much hated each other at school, but now that the bonds and restraints of such a tired institutional set-up were banished from our young lives, we could go about constructing some form of connection.

She passed me in the main reception as I entered the station. I went to say hello, but she was already gone – possibly from my day altogether. Would there be another opportunity to see her again today? This drew the air from my lungs, the strength from my legs. I thought about going after her, then decided against it. I sat down and mulled things over. Then, she walked past again, heading back the way she'd come. I stood up and stepped towards her.

'Lucy,' I greeted her, 'hi!'

'Hi,' she said back, carrying on her way. She pushed the double doors ahead of her open and stepped through. I followed beside her, covertly drawing in her scent when proximity permitted. 'What do you want?' she asked, stopping and turning to face me.

'Good question,' was all I could respond with. She rolled her eyes and carried on. 'Actually, I, erm,' I thought, her pace difficult to allow thinking time. 'I was wondering if you wanted to, you know...'

'No, I don't know,' she responded indifferently, reaching Inspector Hastings' door.

'Go out with me.' I took the plunge. All she did was laugh in my face, before knocking on the door.

'Come in,' Hastings called out, and she did so, closing the door in my face. At once I was again plucked away and thrown down further along my life.

* * *

I walked into the hallway. It was dark, the curtains still drawn. I opened them and walked into the living room. Words cannot describe the sight that awaited me. There was Lucy, sprawled on the carpet and covered in blood. She was naked, her battered body left in a heap like a discarded pile of rubble. I dropped to my knees, weeping, shaking her and begging her to wake up.

* * *

The police had me lined up as her killer, and this was too much to contend with. I became cold, uncooperative and disruptive to their neat plans for a tidy case. Noose was the only one who believed me, for no other reason than he just did; but he had his own problems. As he was leading me through the police reception one day during investigations, his wife and their young son charged in and began yelling abuse at him.

'How could you do this to your family?' she was screeching, the tears flowing and her face bright red. She was certainly older than her husband, and looked rather drawn and lifeless with it too. There was something not altogether sincere about her tears. Indeed, why had she come to Noose's place of work to have this argument? 'Where is she then?' she went on.

'Go away Sam, I'm working.'

'Look,' she carried on, yanking at her son's arm and pushing him at Noose. 'Just look at what you're ruining for a quick fling with that slut Nicola.' The boy looked up at his father, puzzled and as angry as his mother.

'Please, we'll have this discussion later. I must get on with Peter's case.'

'Ah, so this is *the* Peter Smith you're so obsessed with, is it? Don't bother coming home, Henry, we're finished.' She stormed off, dragging the boy with her.

'But, Sam, wait,' he called back.

She turned back in the doorway, shouting: 'Always about the job with you, never about your family. Well, you enjoy yourself. Poor Gary doesn't even know who his father is these days. He never sees you now, and he never will again.' She left, the door swinging open and shut for nearly a minute afterwards due to her force.

'Bit awkward, that,' I said to Noose, trying to look sympathetic. I was not really in the mood for sympathy – nobody had shown me any – but this sergeant had at least shown me some form of care and interest. I tried desperately to block all the hurt and torment from my mind. Lucy was everything to me, I just had to make her nothing or her senseless and barbaric murder would be my undoing. I was good at forgetting and making everything nothing.

* * *

You, the reader of my memoirs or whatever they are, needn't be made privy to my current placing as I write this – all you need to know is that I am catapulted into an unfathomable place so distant that it is neither in the future nor past and I remember everything about all my prior existences. Did I ever make old age? Was I eternally reborn throughout history with diminishing returns? I have been a child so many times and I have been a young adult so many times as years, and human existence, have trundled on. I have also been trapped endlessly in what should only be described as my final life. My final life, or lives, beginning with my birth in the year 1975, is so vast and complex as to herniate even the most advanced mind. The reasons for being held back from moving on to the next life, as per the routine of The Space's gift, were to provide me with my only chance of living a full singular life – with the woman who was waiting to be by my side. However, I had not bargained for Reaping Icon and his games, least of all with the removal of my memory at his whim. He is that niggle at the back of your conscience pushing you to cruelty – pushing you to the sad truth about humanity. With the power to close The Space off from humanity and thus end our curse lying on my shoulders alone, I was the final link between The Great Collective and The Space. The problem was, I didn't know it. I am not living, I am dead. I am existing in an endless cycle of cruelty. To cease this incessant routine is to live.

Hello. My name is Peter Smith. I am dead.

was a lot smaller with a bustling attitude always walking around with a duster looking for something to dust.

They owned both properties and their son Bryan lived in the flats above the shops with his wife and young daughter. Bryan was very much the businessman of the family and did the majority of the buying and promoting with his wife attending to the bookkeeping. I got the impression that he looked on his mother and father as being more of a retirement couple passing the time in the shop, I think Mr Hickman senior had different ideas.

Behind the counter was an annexe which led out to the long garden for the flat above. The annexe was where most of the packing was done for their very busy mail order and export side of the business.

There was also a second china shop around the corner in Duke Street. This was run by two ladies Jennie and Ruth. It sold the same china goods and had the same style of cellar as well.

The morning was mainly spent with Bob showing me around the shop and introducing me to the hundreds of different makes of china and ornaments for sale. This is where I got my liking for Coalport, Border Fine Arts, Lilliput Lane, Wedgewood, Port Merion and far too many more to list here.

Lunchtime arrived and I made my way up to the Row Barge pub behind the fire station for a bite to eat. This became a regular event most days. I only had half an hour and so phoned ahead to order my food and it would be hot and waiting on the bar by the time I had made the 5 min walk up the hill.

That afternoon I was in the annexe learning how to complete the export and VAT exempt paperwork with Bryan when my alerter went off. I jumped, Bryan jumped, and I began to move,

This cellar had a musty damp smell which wasn't surprising as with the river Thames only a stone's throw down the high street, we were very near to the water table level. What I loved down there was the fact that the whole building had been constructed from recycled Thames barges. The solid oak beams that had been reused still had the original cuts and fixings from when the plied their trade many years ago along the river. I've always been a huge fan of history, which was seriously fuelled by my history teacher Mrs Pam Syrett and form teacher, also a history teacher Mr Bob Phillips, both of whom I remained in touch with, in my adult years. Both have now sadly passed. I was able to go to Mrs Syrett's funeral, and it is testament to her popularity that a large number of ex pupils turned up to say goodbye to her.

The first thing I was shown was where to make the tea and who had what. Get the important things over first.

As the morning was very quiet, we sat down and Mr Hickman, Bob, asked me how my previous three weeks had gone. This was a family business, Mr Hickman was a tall elderly man in his early 60s with straggly and thinning grey hair. He was somewhat overweight and almost always wore a brown leather jacket. He had a way of showing interest in what you had been doing to pass conversation, but I could see he very quickly would get bored, and you would lose his attention very easily. His wife